NO HOLDS BARRED

BY
CARA SUMMERS

MILLS
BOON

First published in Great Britain 2012
by Mills & Boon, an imprint of Harlequin (UK) Limited,
Eton House, 18-24 Paradise Road, Richmond, Surrey TW9 1SR

© Carolyn Hanlon 2012

ISBN: 978 0 263 89741 8

30-0912

Was **Cara Summers** born with the dream of becoming a published romance novelist? No. But now that she is, she still feels her dream has come true. And she owes it all to her mother, who handed her a romance novel years ago and said, "Try it. You'll love it." Mom was right! Cara has written over forty stories for Blaze, and she has won numerous awards including a Lifetime Achievement Award for Series Storyteller of the Year from *RT Book Review*s. When she isn't working on new books, she teaches in the writing program at Syracuse University.

To my grandchildren, Marian and Andrew.
All my love for the future.

Prologue

Glen Loch, New York, Summer, 1812

ELEANOR CAMPBELL MACPHERSON stood on the cliffs alone, except for her memories. And there were so many good ones. In a marriage that had lasted over fifty years, she and Angus had come here so often. The caves below in the cliff face had always been one of their secret places. They'd picnicked there often during the early years of their marriage, sometimes climbing up from the lake below and sometimes climbing down. And later, after the children and even the grandchildren had arrived, it had been one of their secret trysting places. Sneaking away to make love here with Angus had always made her feel wicked and wild and very like the young girl who had allowed him to sweep her away all those many years ago.

She missed him so much. How often had they walked together here on mornings just like this one?

The mists swirled over the lake, but the newly risen sun, a bright red ball, would burn them away quickly. To the west on a rocky promontory stood Castle MacPherson, the home that Angus had built for them.

There it rose, three stories high, strong and graceful and as enduring as the life they'd built together. Beyond it she saw the gardens that gave her so much pleasure. And at the far edge, nestled at the foot of a sharply rising hillside, she could make out the top of the stone arch that Angus had built for her.

It was a replica of an older arch that had stood in the gardens of her family's estate in Scotland and it had a legendary power from ancient times—the power to unite true lovers. The story had been passed down for years in the Campbell clan—the man or the woman you kissed beneath the stone arch would be your true love forever. Angus had even stolen some of the stones from the original arch so that this one would carry the same power.

With a smile, Eleanor let her mind drift back to that long ago night when she and Angus had met beneath those powerful stones on the Campbell estate for the last time. Her family had thrown a ball to celebrate her upcoming wedding, and she'd been wearing her future husband's gift to her—a sapphire necklace and earrings that had been bestowed on his family for service to the Scottish court. Mary Stuart had worn the jewels at her coronation, and Eleanor's husband-to-be had insisted that she wear them at their betrothal ball as proof of his love for her.

She'd snuck out of the ball to meet with Angus and to tell him that their secret meetings had to end. She'd practiced the speech for days. There was no future for them. Their families had been locked in a blood feud for years. She was promised to another man, a fine man from a prominent family. Then Angus had kissed her the moment she'd arrived—before she could say a word.

And that had been that.

Oh, she'd tried to talk some sense into him, but he wouldn't listen. Impetuous, impatient, irresistible, Angus hadn't taken no for an answer. He'd simply promised her everything and carried her away.

Thank God.

Eleanor let her gaze linger on the castle, with its lovely gardens and the stone arch. Angus had delivered on his promise. He'd given her everything. Going with him and settling here was the best decision she'd ever made. She only had one regret. And that was what had brought her to the cliffs this morning.

Slipping her hand into her pocket, she closed it over the leather pouches that held the Stuart Sapphires. Having them had always troubled her conscience. A man who'd loved her had given them to her. Not only had she betrayed that love, she'd also become a thief. Everything had happened so fast the night she'd fled with Angus, and any attempt at sending the jewels back later might have given her family some clue as to what she'd done, where she was. It was better that she just vanish.

But Angus had always known about her feelings. It was why he was visiting her now in her dreams, helping her to make things right. He'd always been so very good at making things right.

The latest dream had come this morning, and it had brought her here to the cliffs. She would tell no one what she was doing. Her sons and her daughters-in-law wouldn't be pleased. They'd always assumed that the sapphire necklace and earrings she'd worn in her wedding portrait had been her dowry, the gift that her family had given to her when she'd married Angus.

The stone arch had played a part in the first dreams that Angus had sent her. In them she'd seen a young girl with reddish-gold curls finding one of the Stuart earrings in the stones. Angus had said her name was Adair. So Eleanor had hidden the first of the earrings there.

But the girl in her latest dream had long dark hair and she'd found the second earring in one of the inner chambers of the caves. Eleanor tightened her grip on the pouch in her pocket, and as she did, she heard Angus's voice in her ear.

Her name is Piper. She believes in the power of the stone arch enough to bury her dreams and fantasies beneath them. And she knows about our secret cave. When she finds the second earring, the Stuart Sapphires will continue to find their way home. Trust me, Ellie...just as you did on the night we ran away.

The mists had cleared from the lake. With Angus's words still clear in her mind, Eleanor began the short climb down the cliff face to the cave, just as she'd done so many times with her lover before. She would leave the second earring for Piper to find, and then she would wait for Angus to send her more dreams.

1

PIPER SNAPPED AWAKE AT THE first annoying clang of her Donald Duck alarm clock. A long-ago birthday present from her sisters. They knew how she loved keeping her life in order and on schedule. Donald had gotten her to class on time through four years of college and three years at Georgetown Law School. He was still going strong. The clock had no batteries, no power source, and all it required to silence it was a strong, determined whack.

She gave it one. And since Donald provided no snooze option, she sat up in bed and rubbed her eyes. Then she ran her hand through her hair and automatically reached for the scrunchy she'd left on her nightstand. Her mind was already clearing and her vision would, too, in a couple of seconds. In the meantime, she tossed off the covers and reached for the gym shorts she always laid out at the foot of the bed. Swinging her legs to the floor, she pulled them on, then groped for the sports bra and T-shirt. By the time she'd managed

socks and her running shoes, she could find her way
to the bathroom to brush her teeth.

Her next stop was the coffeemaker in her kitchen.
Unlike Donald, it required a power source, and thanks
to top-of-the-line technology, it had already brewed a
pot of strong coffee. The coffeemaker had also been a
gift from her sisters. She poured a quarter of a cup and
inhaled the fumes while she stretched and then slipped
on the wristlet that held her apartment key. Finally, she
took her cell phone off its charger and slipped it into
her pocket.

Her morning routine never varied. But then variety wasn't her goal. Order and routine were. Life got
messy. Piper had learned at an early age that control-
ling the parts she could gave her more time to fix up
the messy ones.

And lately, her professional life had gotten very
messy.

Not yet. Firmly, she blocked the thought while she
blew on the coffee and managed two swallows that
burned her mouth and nearly cauterized her throat.
It was a sacrifice she made each morning to the caffeine goddess.

Then she headed for the door of the flat she leased
above a ritzy women's clothing boutique in Georgetown, shut the door, tested the lock, then hurried down
the steps and along the short alley to the sidewalk. At
6:00 a.m., the street was still mostly free of traffic. Mr.
Findley who ran the coffee shop down the street was
washing his windows, while a customer sat at one of
the outside tables reading a paper. The sun was up and
the humidity tolerable. The scent of stale beer and fresh
bread baking mingled in the still air. Perfect.

She ran because it was an ingrained habit from her

high school and college years, when she'd been on cross-country teams. But she also ran because it was the best way she knew to clear her mind and get ready to face the day.

Which promised to be another busy one. Her current job as a research assistant to prominent law professor and celebrity defense attorney Abraham Monticello was one she worked hard at. She'd accepted his offer right out of law school because it would look good on her résumé and because it offered her a unique chance to get a background in criminal law.

It was turning out to be unique, all right, and it was causing her to question her career choice. Her main reason for choosing law as a profession was that she believed in justice and in the power of the legal system to help people find it. But recently....

No. Not yet.

While she took the first block at an easy pace, she used a visualization technique her aunt Vi had taught her when she was very young. First, she pictured all the chaos of her upcoming day and her self-doubts being sucked into a bottle in much the same way Aladdin's genie had been sucked into the lamp. Then she jammed the cork in with the same energy she'd used to whack Donald.

Whenever things got really bad, she let herself remember the really chaotic time in her life right after her mother died. She'd been three, her older sister Adair four, and Nell had been a baby. They'd been too young to really understand the loss—except that their mother wasn't there anymore. And neither was their father. He'd hidden away in his studio and used his art to escape from his grief. Then their Aunt Vi had moved into the castle with them, and life had finally taken on some order again. That's probably when her love of routine had taken root.

As she reached the end of the second block, Piper shifted her focus to the details of her surroundings, taking the opportunity to speed window-shop in the stores that stretched along the street. She saw changes in the displays and made a mental note to take a closer look at a pair of red sandals—when she had the time. And she'd have to *make* time to call Nell and tell her that her first published children's book, *It's All Good,* was still on display in the window of the bookstore.

When her younger sister had last visited, she'd made a good friend of the owner and now Nell's story was selling well in Georgetown. Piper had to admit she was impressed. Nell had inherited their father's creative talent, except she'd chosen writing rather than landscape painting as A. D. MacPherson had.

But she certainly hadn't inherited their father's reticence. Currently, Nell was using a federal grant to travel across the country, offering writing classes to children in underprivileged schools, and at the same time, establishing a network for her own writing.

As Piper turned down a residential street, her muscles began to warm and perspiration sheened on her forehead. She settled into a rhythm. If Nell was surprising her, her older sister Adair had truly shocked her.

During the past eight months, Adair and their aunt Vi had turned Castle MacPherson, their family home in the Adirondacks, into what was becoming a very successful wedding destination spot. Adair had always been an idea person, and when they'd been growing up, Piper and Nell had been more than willing to go along with most of her schemes. But whenever Adair's plans had gone awry, it had always been Piper's job to do the cleanup, which usually included negotiating with Aunt Vi, and on some occasions, even with their father.

No wonder she'd always been drawn to the practice of law. What did lawyers do except clean up the messes people got themselves into?

Only this time, the mess was of her own making.

Not yet. She was not going there yet.

The biggest surprise from the castle was that her sister and Aunt Vi had discovered one piece of their several-times-great grandmother, Eleanor Campbell MacPherson's, priceless missing dowry: a sapphire earring that had reputedly been worn by Mary Stuart on the day she'd taken the throne. And during the same weekend, Aunt Vi had gotten engaged to Daryl Garnett, who ran the domestic operations unit of the CIA here in D.C. Even more astounding was that Adair, the practical queen of the five-year plan, had fallen in love, too. With Cam Sutherland, of all people.

Piper ran in place at the corner until the traffic cleared, then found her stride again. She hadn't seen any of the Sutherland triplets since her father had married their mother seven years ago. The MacPherson sisters and the Sutherland triplets, Reid, Cameron and Duncan, went back a long way to a summer of play-dates when the boys had opened up a whole new world of games—bad guys versus good guys, sheriff and posse, pirates and treasure, along with rock-climbing on the cliff face, a place where she and her sisters had been forbidden to play.

Then the Sutherlands had completely disappeared from their lives until they'd returned to the castle on the day their mother, Professor Beth Sutherland, married A. D. MacPherson beneath the stone arch. Since she had an eye for detail, Piper had duly noted that the scruffy, annoying Sutherland boys had morphed into tall, gorgeous and hot young men.

Especially one of them. Duncan. He'd really caught her attention that day with that tall, rangy body, the dark unruly hair and the mesmerizing green eyes. She'd felt those eyes on her during the ceremony when they'd been standing with their parents beneath the stone arch, and she'd felt a kind of tingly awareness that rippled along her nerve endings and heightened all of her other senses.

Intrigued, she'd met his gaze directly, and for a span of time, her vision and her mind had been totally filled with him and nothing else. Only Duncan. Heat had flooded her, melting her, muscle and bone, right to her core. The experience had been so new, so exciting, so terrifying. No one had ever made her feel that way before—or since.

Not that she'd had to worry about it. The triplets had flown in for the wedding and had returned to their respective colleges that night. She and her sisters had done the same the next day. Just as well. A man like Duncan Sutherland would likely wreak havoc on a girl's life, something she didn't have time for. She had enough problems to deal with in her work life.

Work. Her mind veered back to the coming day.

No. Not yet.

Increasing her pace, Piper ran full out for the next two blocks—pushing herself into a zone where all she had to do was enjoy the speed and the wind whipping past her face. The next corner marked the halfway point of her run. As she circled to head back, she moved into a slower rhythm and allowed herself to finally uncork the work bottle and face her demons.

Mentally, she made a list, one she'd been making

almost every day lately. Good news first. She loved working for Abe Monticello, and up until a few months ago, she'd loved everything about the job. The only irritation she'd had to face was one of her fellow research assistants, Richard Starkweather. He wanted to date her and was having difficulty taking no for an answer. But she could handle that.

And working for Abe Monticello was more than worth a minor hassle with a colleague. He was a larger-than-life man with a larger-than-average talent. At sixty-five, he had the sharpness of mind, the looks and the creative imagination of a man half his age. If he'd *been* half his age and unmarried, Piper might have fallen in love with him.

Everything had been perfect until Abe had been hired to handle the appeal in a highly publicized case. It involved a man on death row who'd been convicted of murdering a young woman, but suspected of killing several others. Many, including the FBI, believed Patrick Lightman was the serial murderer the press had dubbed the RPK, or the Rose Petal Killer.

Piper had been thrilled when Abe had assigned her to do the research for the appeal and write a brief. She'd worked on Lightman's case for two straight months. She'd studied the court recordings, read the media coverage and she'd viewed the crime scene photos of Suzanne Macks, the woman he'd been arrested for killing. Her killer had taken the time to arrange a little picnic setting. A white sheet had been spread across the floor of the living room of her apartment. Suzanne had been lying on top of it, her eyes closed, her hands folded across her chest and her long dark hair fanned out from her head. Rose petals, hundreds of them, had been strewn everywhere.

The Rose Petal Killer had left all of his victims exactly that way.

Everyone had believed Lightman guilty. The jury had taken only an hour to bring in a verdict.

But Piper had uncovered exactly what her boss had been hoping for—several procedural errors in the trial. She'd done the job and she'd done it well, but the hardest thing she'd ever done in her life was to hand her findings, along with the brief, over to her boss. Then a month ago, Abe had used what she'd written to successfully argue the case before the appeals court. And Patrick Lightman had been set free.

A man who'd been convicted of viciously murdering a young woman and who might very well have murdered seven others was walking the streets and could possibly kill again. Piper figured it was the biggest mess she'd ever gotten herself into.

For a couple of weeks, the media had created a circus surrounding the release of the Rose Petal Killer. Abe had taken all the heat. He was the one who'd received hate mail.

But she was the one who had the nightmares. In them, she pictured Patrick Lightman out on the streets, following another young girl with long dark hair. If Lightman was the Rose Petal Killer, he could even now be selecting his next victim. And Piper would be responsible.

Abe had taken the time to have a heart-to-heart talk with her. He'd reiterated his belief in the basic right of every citizen to a vigorous defense. The law always had to be applied meticulously and fairly in order to ensure justice. Piper believed that, too. In theory. But she was discovering there was a world of difference between theory and practice. What if Patrick Lightman killed again?

The only answer Abe had on that one was that prosecutors and defense attorneys couldn't afford to let the job get personal. Then he'd encouraged her to throw herself into the next case, one he was set to argue in court within the next month, and he'd invited her to sit in the second chair. It meant more work, but it would get her mind off Patrick Lightman. Just what Abe had intended it to do.

Time to put it all back in the bottle. Picturing the process once again in her mind, Piper turned the final corner and sprinted for the entrance of her alleyway. At least the reporters had never bugged her at home. Piper took the stairs to her apartment two at a time. If she hadn't let her mind wander back to work, she might have been more aware of her surroundings. As it was, her feet were both planted on the landing before she fully registered that the door to her apartment was open. In fact, it had been propped open with the ladder-back chair from her kitchen table.

By that time, she'd glanced into the room and what she saw froze her to the spot. Hysteria bubbled into her throat and blocked a scream. Someone had staged the scene perfectly. Her coffee table had been shoved to the side. A white sheet had been thrown across the floor the way a picnic blanket might be spread across a patch of lawn. Strewn across the white cloth were hundreds of rose petals. Enough to appear as if they'd rained out of the sky. And red enough to look like blood.

The only thing that was missing was the body of a young woman with long brown hair, her hands crossed over her chest, the scene she'd pictured several times in her nightmares.

Piper pressed a hand against her chest. She had to think. She had to breathe. And she had to get away from here. Still, she wasn't sure how long it took her to tear her gaze away from the rose petals and get down the flight of stairs. She ran then, and she didn't stop to use her cell phone until she'd dashed into the coffee shop down the street.

IT WAS DUNCAN SUTHERLAND'S day off, and to make sure he enjoyed every minute of it, he'd scheduled a 7:00 a.m. tee-off time. Although he preferred a low-key, laid-back approach to life, there were some deadlines that had to be met. And a tee-off time was sacred. Plus, he needed a break from work. Ever since accused serial killer Patrick Lightman had been set free, Duncan had been reviewing the FBI's files during every minute of his spare time. He'd been the lead profiler on Lightman, and he was determined to put the man back in jail. There had to be something in the files that had been overlooked, some detail or angle that he hadn't seen yet.

The first phone call came just as he was about to step into the shower.

A quick look at the caller ID told him it was bad news. His brother Cam never called except to report trouble or ask a favor. Either one might interfere with the perfect day he had planned. Cam's last call had been a favor. Duncan had transported a veterinarian from Montana to upstate New York to reunite him with his ex-wife.

He let the phone ring four times, then gave up and answered. "Trouble or favor?"

Cam laughed.

So it would be a favor. "I'm teeing off in an hour,"

Duncan warned. "And what time is it in Scotland any-way?" His brother had taken some time from his job at the CIA to run off to Scotland with Adair MacPherson. They'd recently become unofficially engaged and they were going to deliver the news in person to their respective parents, who were both on a working vacation there.

"Relax. I just wanted to know if you'd given any more thought to going up to Castle MacPherson and poking around in the library?"

"Some." Cam had been nagging him about that ever since he'd shown him the sapphire earring that Adair and Vi had discovered in the stone arch. His brother believed that someone had been sneaking into Castle MacPherson for nearly six months, and they still had no idea who the intruder was. But the nocturnal visits had started right about the time the *New York Times* had run a feature article on the castle and those missing jewels that Mary Stuart had reputedly worn at her coronation. Cam's theory was that the visitations had something to do with the missing jewels. That would have been his own best guess.

"You're the profiler in the family," Cam said. "If anybody can get some handle on who the intruder was, it's you. You always had a knack for getting into people's heads."

As the youngest of triplets, Duncan supposed that he'd developed that knack as a survival skill. And it had been part of what had drawn him to the FBI's Behavioral Analysis Unit. The other part of it had been what had drawn all three of them into some kind of law enforcement—the arrest of their father for embezzlement. They'd been nine when it had happened, and Duncan still carried the image in his mind of the three of them standing in front of their mother as the police handcuffed their father and led him away. Duncan also remembered what he'd felt—a fierce kind of happiness that David Fedderman couldn't hurt their mother anymore.

"He's still out there," Cam continued. "And the rest of Eleanor's dowry has to be at the castle somewhere. You don't want to miss out on a chance to find it, do you?"

It was Duncan's turn to laugh. As the middle triplet, Cam had always felt the need to compete, especially with Reid, the first born. "You should try that 'miss out on a chance' tactic with Reid. You could always get him with it when we were kids."

"I intend to," Cam said. "But serving on the vice president's Secret Service detail is keeping him hopping. Besides, the strategy will work more effectively after *you* find either the necklace or the other earring. Help me out here."

"Not on your life. My philosophy has always been to not take sides when it comes to the two of you and your competition." Waiting it out until the dust settled had always worked well for him.

"It was worth a shot. But you can't tell me that you don't want to find part of Eleanor's dowry. You were fascinated by those sapphires when you were a kid."

A brother, especially one with CIA training, knew what buttons to push. The truth was Duncan had been thinking about visiting the castle. The summer he was ten and they'd had daily playdates with the MacPherson girls, he'd spent hours studying Eleanor's wedding portrait, and he'd memorized the legendary jewels. Two thumbnail-sized sapphires hung from each earring and one of the jewels on the necklace rivaled the Hope Diamond in size.

There was a story there that hadn't been told. Tradition held that the jewels had been Eleanor's dowry, but there was no record of what had happened to them until the first earring had shown up less than a month ago when lightning had struck the stone arch and loosened some stones. Someone had hidden it. Who? And why? Those were the questions that drove all of his investigations.

"So—will you go?" Cam prodded.

Duncan shifted his thoughts back to the conversation and stalled. "I thought that you and Adair had run off to Scotland to see what you could dig up about the sapphires on that end."

"That's our plan, but the rest of Eleanor's dowry is at the castle. And I still think there's something in that library that holds the key."

Once again, he had to agree with Cam's assessment. The security had been beefed up at the castle, and the local sheriff was sending regular patrols now.

"The air is a lot fresher up there than it is in that basement you work in at Quantico," Cam said. "It'll be fairly quiet. No wedding is scheduled, just a photo shoot for some fancy architecture magazine. Daryl will be visiting Vi on the weekend. The two of you might be able to get in a game of golf."

Daryl Garnett was Cam's boss at the CIA and he'd recently become engaged to Vi. He was also a scratch golfer. Leave it to a brother to know your weaknesses. Duncan glanced at his watch. The minutes to his tee time were slipping away.

"If I tell you I'm planning on going up there this

weekend, will you go back to your fiancée and our parents and leave me alone?"

"You've got it, bro. My job with you is done," Cam said, and clicked off.

It wasn't until Duncan was stepping out of the shower a few minutes later that the second call came. And it meant he'd have to cancel his tee time and perhaps even his trip to the castle. There was a chance that the Rose Petal Killer had selected a new victim.

2

DUNCAN SHOWED HIS BADGE TO THE young uniformed officer standing on the landing of the small apartment then ducked his head to step inside. The space was small—one room where a minimum of furniture had been artfully arranged to separate the eating area from the living space. The floor between the couch and fireplace was completely covered by a white sheet sprinkled liberally with bloodred rose petals very much in the style of the Rose Petal Killer.

He'd get back to that in a moment. For now he took in the other details. A tiny kitchen was tucked into an alcove and a door directly ahead led into a bedroom the size of a closet. No surprise that the place was so crowded, considering all the people in it. Two of the men he didn't recognize. They were carefully dusting surfaces for prints. The other two he knew on sight. They stood just inside the bedroom. One was Detective Mike Nelson, who'd given him the call when he'd stepped out of the shower. Duncan had consulted on a case of Mike's the year he'd been hired to work at Quantico and they'd been friends ever since. The other man he recognized as Abe Monticello, whose head, like his own, was nearly brushing the ceiling. He was the reason that Duncan had missed his golf game.

Abe hadn't called him personally; instead, he'd called his sister, who happened to be Duncan's boss.

It had been a rough month for Adrienne Monticello. The division she commanded at Quantico had worked on the Rose Petal Killer cases, and her brother had been responsible for setting Patrick Lightman loose. Since she considered Duncan to be the division's expert on the RPK, Adrienne had asked him to go over to Georgetown and give her his personal take on the scene. Mike Nelson had called him, too, and asked if he could stop by.

It didn't surprise him at all that Abe Monticello had wanted the FBI involved in this from the get-go. He was a smart man and very savvy about handling the press. Someone had broken into the apartment of one of his research assistants and staged a scene that matched the romantic little sets that the Rose Petal Killer had designed for his victims. Abe would want to step into his favorite role—the white knight, charging in to save the day.

Both Adrienne and Nelson had called him because they wanted the answer to one question. Was this the work of the real Rose Petal Killer or a copycat? He imagined Nelson would prefer the former. The detective, along with everyone else in law enforcement, would like to get Lightman back behind bars.

Abe Monticello wanted the answer to be "copycat" because he'd spent a lot of time in front of TV cameras during the past few weeks speaking in defense of the legal system and the way it worked to prevent the violation of every citizen's rights. The speech might not play so well if Patrick Lightman started murdering slender young brunettes again. Or threatening to.

Well, you couldn't please everyone, and Duncan already had a feeling about which man would be happier about his opinion. His insights into the criminal mind were usually right. His mother had told him when he'd joined the FBI that his interest in behavioral science had begun with his trying to figure out what had motivated his father to become an embezzler.

David Fedderman had been born to wealth and privilege, but he'd abused both. In his position at Fedderman Investments, a firm that his grandfather had founded, he'd run a successful Ponzi scheme for years until it had collapsed and Fedderman had been arrested on several counts of fraud.

Of course, his father's arrest and eventual incarceration hadn't been the end of the story. His mother had had to battle Fedderman's parents for custody, and as soon as she'd won, she'd legally changed all their names back to Sutherland and accepted a position teaching at a liberal arts college in Chicago. As to figuring his father out, that hadn't been much of a challenge. David Fedderman had been one of those men for whom running a con and living life on a constant adrenaline rush was worth more than family or wealth. It had been worth risking everything. He was still serving time in a federal prison, and Duncan would have bet good money his father was still running scams.

Analyzing what he was seeing in front of him was a lot more challenging. The way the white sheet was spread was fairly accurate, the edges folded in to make what looked like a perfect square. The Rose Petal Killer had been meticulous about that. In the tiny room, the sheet filled most of the available space between the couch and a TV stand against one wall. Duncan dropped to one knee and caught the edge of the sheet between his thumb and his forefinger and rubbed. Then he studied the rose petals. They all looked fairly fresh.

Nelson spotted him first and walked to the back of the sofa. "Thanks for coming, Sutherland. Take your time."

He didn't need any more time to answer the question he figured was foremost in Mike's mind, but he'd learned a long time ago that the information he provided would be taken more seriously if he strategically delayed the delivery. "Any sign of a break-in?" he asked.

"No. She was out for a run when it happened. Claims she locked the door and took the key," Nelson said. "The only person who has a spare key is the woman who runs the dress shop downstairs. We'll question her as soon as she opens up."

The lack of evidence of a break-in was consistent with the RPK's pattern. The widely accepted theory was that his victims let him in. But that hadn't happened in this case.

"We didn't find any evidence that the lock was picked," Nelson continued. "But a pro wouldn't have had a problem with it."

And a duplicate key made from a wax impression was also a possibility, Duncan mused. A robbery ring recently arrested in nearby Baltimore had accessed house keys by distracting parking valets at high-end restaurants. The customers would return home after an evening of fine dining to find their houses stripped. A stalker with the patience and skills of Patrick Lightman might have used a similar method to gain access to his victims' homes.

It was when he was replacing the edge of the sheet that Duncan spotted the thin envelope that lay just beneath. He pinched the corner of it to draw it out.

"I want to know if Ms. MacPherson is in danger," Monticello said.

As Duncan glanced up and met the older man's eyes, his mind was racing. "Ms. MacPherson?" Piper wasn't a common name and he recalled that Piper MacPherson had gotten her law degree from Georgetown Law School.

"Yes," Abe said. "She works for me. I want to know just how much danger she's in."

Abe hadn't mentioned her first name yet, but Duncan was beginning to get a feeling. Then Piper strode into the room and confirmed it in spades.

He hadn't seen her in seven years, not since they'd stood beneath the stone arch at the castle and listened to their parents exchange vows. But every detail of her appearance slammed into his mind and pummeled his senses. The slender frame, the long, long legs that extended from narrow ankles to running shorts, the compact curves, slim waist and the dark brown hair that hung in a ponytail. He'd never been so aware of a woman as he'd been the day of the wedding. Or now.

"Whoever did this isn't the Rose Petal Killer," she said as she walked with economical grace toward Nelson and Monticello.

The voice with its low pitch and huskiness rippled along his nerve endings. It was the kind of voice that tempted a man to come closer. A whole lot closer. He imagined the mythical sirens who'd lured sailors to their deaths might have had voices exactly like hers. Which was why he'd kept his distance on their parents' wedding day. He'd been about to graduate from college and had his sights set on the FBI. And their parents' marriage had made the MacPherson girls family.

"Of course it's not," Abe Monticello said.

"The FBI is here to determine that for us," Nelson said.

Duncan stayed right where he was. For a moment he still needed the distance, but he knew the second she became aware of him. He could see the tension ripple through her, and even as she turned, he braced himself. Seven years was still a long time.

But as he looked into those amazing amber-colored eyes, once again he felt the impact like a blow. Desire sprang up, primitive and strong enough to nearly have him rising from his crouch. Then he felt his mind empty as suddenly as if someone had pulled a plug. All he could see was her. All he wanted was her.

For seven years, he'd tried to convince himself that what he'd felt that day was a fluke. A onetime event. And he'd succeeded in compartmentalizing it.

But he knew now exactly what he'd known then. Piper MacPherson was it for him. The only one. For seven years he'd compartmentalized that, too. He'd tried to convince himself that she was family, and that meant hands-off. But as he continued to sink into the depths of those golden eyes, Duncan had a feeling that the lids on all those compartments had been blown clean off.

"You," she said.

In Duncan's opinion, she'd summed up his situation nicely. And what in the hell was he going to do about it?

PIPER CLOSED HER EYES. There was always the chance that she was hallucinating. Or her habit of visualizing was getting the best of her. But when she opened her eyes again, Duncan Sutherland was still crouched on the floor of her apartment.

For an instant, she certainly hoped it wasn't longer than that. She felt just as she had when she'd stopped short in the open doorway of her apartment and seen the rose petals strewn over the white sheet.

Except that it wasn't just shock she was feeling. And her blood hadn't turned to ice. Instead, it seemed to be sizzling through her veins like an electrical current, melting bones and paralyzing muscles so that she wasn't sure she could talk. Or move.

"What are you doing here?" she asked.

"This is FBI agent Duncan Sutherland, Ms. MacPherson," Mike Nelson said. "He works for the Behavioral Analysis Unit at Quantico. I asked him here because he worked on the Rose Petal killings."

"I know Duncan," Piper said. Okay, she was breathing and talking. In a couple of seconds, she'd get her thoughts back on track. Should she try stuffing him into a bottle? Would he fit?

A young uniformed officer appeared in the open doorway. "Sorry, sir. She got away from me."

Piper managed to drag her eyes away from Duncan and glanced back at Nelson. "He was kind enough to get me coffee, and the caffeine helped me think." And she *was* thinking again. Finally. She waved a hand at the sheet. "I came up here to save you some time, Detective. This isn't the work of the Rose Petal Killer."

"Tell me why not," Duncan said.

Bracing herself, Piper turned to face him and managed to take one step closer to the edge of the sheet. And him. "Because the rose petals are so fresh. I read all the files. He used to buy the flowers over the course of days and save them up."

"Too many roses purchased at one time, one place, might have drawn attention. Plus, there was some speculation that he bought them over time as little anonymous gifts for his victims," Duncan said. "And if they saved them, he used those older petals."

She narrowed her eyes. She'd read those very words in the files she'd worked on. And those details had never been released to the press nor had they made it into the court records. Duncan had worked on the cases, all right. Of course he had. He might even have consulted with the police on the Suzanne Macks murder.

"What else is different?" Duncan asked. "Take your time."

She shifted her gaze to the sheet. "I should have done that instead of panicking." She sank to her knees to get a better look. But what she was looking at and what she was feeling were two different things. She was close enough to touch him now. She could certainly smell him—sunshine and soap and something else that bumped up that sizzle in her blood.

Focus.

Ruthlessly, she shifted her attention fully to the details she'd only glanced at before. The edges of the sheet were tucked in to form a perfect square in the available space. That was right. No wrinkles. The RPK had always been neat and precise.

Suddenly, she frowned. "There are fold marks in the sheet, as if it's been newly purchased."

"Good point," Duncan said. "What else?"

Lifting the edge of the sheet, she rubbed it between her thumb and forefinger. "This is wrong, too. The texture is too rough. The thread count should be higher. He always used Egyptian cotton."

"You did read the files," Duncan murmured. "You worked on the appeals brief, didn't you?"

After taking in a deep breath, Piper met his eyes and nodded. She'd prepared herself to find anger, maybe condemnation, censure at the very least. And why not? She'd set a killer free. And now she was facing a man who'd probably worked very hard to bring that killer to justice. But what she saw in the clear green depths of Duncan's eyes was understanding.

Something moved through her then, something she couldn't begin to name. But even as her gaze lingered on his, those green eyes darkened and triggered very different feelings. The rush of desire, the flood of heat, was intense and immediate, as if a button had been pushed. The impulse burst into her mind of just grabbing him, shoving him onto that sheet and rolling with him across it as she stripped him out of those clothes.

No. That couldn't happen.

But the thrill of what that might be like mingled with the accompanying shock that she'd actually thought of doing it. Wanted so badly to do it.

Here.

Now.

If they'd just been alone.

But they weren't. She dragged her gaze away from him and back to the sheet with its bloodred petals. What in the world was wrong with her? No man had ever made her think this...crazily before.

"Ms. MacPherson did an amazing job on the appeal," Abe Monticello was saying. "I've invited her to take second chair in the trial I'm scheduled for in a couple of weeks."

"She did an excellent job," Duncan agreed. "Thanks to her, a shoddy lab was shut down. For a while, our hardworking law enforcement agencies will be very careful about the way they collect and store evidence, and judges will think more precisely about what kind of evidence to admit into the record."

"Before we throw a ticker-tape parade, let's remember that the amazing appeal set a serial killer loose on the streets," Nelson added.

"So put him back in jail," Abe said. "In any case, our experts seem to agree that this incident is the work of a copycat."

"Not so fast. Before we jump on that bandwagon, we'd better take a look at this." Duncan lifted his hand, and out of the corner of her eye, Piper saw the thin envelope he held between two fingers.

"I found this tucked under the sheet." As he spoke he opened the unsealed flap and pulled out a piece of cream-colored vellum, the kind that a formal announcement might have been printed on.

He turned it so that she could see what was written in block letters. THE NEXT TIME, YOU'LL BE THE ONE LYING BENEATH THE PETALS.

It was only as Duncan read the message aloud to the other two men that the meaning began to sink in. A sliver of fear worked its way up her spine, but a little flare of anger chased it away. She shot to her feet. "Leaving a note was never part of the RPK's pattern. Who would do this?"

"Someone who's angry because we won our appeal," Abe said. "So it's clearly not Patrick Lightman. He's got to be very happy with the work we did."

"Well, someone definitely isn't," Nelson muttered.

"Agreed. Your job is to find out who's threatening Ms. MacPherson," Monticello said.

Duncan rose to his feet, but whatever he might have

added was forestalled by the commotion at the door of her apartment. Turning, she saw her colleague Richard Starkweather stride through the still-open door.

"Piper, thank God you're all right." He started toward her.

Duncan quickly stepped in front of her. "Who are you?"

Richard frowned at him. "Who are you?"

"He's all right," Abe said. "Richard Starkweather is one of my research assistants."

Because Duncan was completely blocking her view, Piper edged to his side. Two men now flanked Richard, a uniformed officer and Detective Nelson.

"What are you doing here?" Nelson asked the question that was foremost in Piper's mind.

"I came to see if Piper was all right. It's all over the news that the Rose Petal Killer has struck again." He gestured toward the petal-strewn sheet. "They're running footage of the crime scene on all three local news stations. It's even posted on YouTube. When I recognized Piper's apartment, I had to come over here to make sure she was all right. Surely you can understand that, Officer."

"Detective," Nelson corrected.

When the TV blared on, Piper turned to see that Abe was using the remote to find a news channel. The moment he did, they were all viewing a video clip of the scene in her apartment. It was exactly what she'd encountered when she'd returned from her run. There was a shot of the room that took in her kitchen, the open door to the bedroom, all the way to the fireplace. Then the picture on the TV screen narrowed to a close-up of the petal-strewn sheet. She felt a sliver of ice work its way up her spine.

A reporter's voice was saying, "This was the scene early this morning when attorney Piper MacPherson returned to her apartment. Our source tells us that Ms. MacPherson worked on the appeal that set accused Rose Petal Killer, Patrick Lightman, free. Will she be his next victim?"

Mike Nelson pulled out his phone. "I'll find out how they got that video clip."

"Whoever set up this little scene could easily have shot it on his cell phone before he left," Duncan said. "Then he could have attached it to an email. Stark-weather just said it's accessible on YouTube."

Abe switched channels and caught another replay of the tape. A reporter gave the same information in a voice-over.

Piper made herself look carefully at it this time. "Someone shot the scene from the open doorway, then stepped inside for the close-up of the sheet. But why would anyone do this?"

There were three full beats of silence before Duncan directed a question to Abe. "Who knows she worked on the brief? So far you've kept a tight lid on that."

"Intentionally," Abe said. "No one from my office leaked it."

"Well, somebody found out," Duncan said. "And whoever did this is angry enough at her to paint a target on her back."

Great, Piper thought. She could picture it clearly in her mind. How could a day that had started out so normally become a nightmare so quickly?

3

Two hours later, Duncan stood in the alley gazing at the wooden staircase that led to Piper's small apartment. Finally, he was alone.

Monticello had left first, waiting only until Piper had showered and changed so that he could personally escort her to work. Most members of the press who'd finally tracked down Piper's apartment had scurried after Abe's limo.

Mike Nelson had lingered longer. His men had talked to Piper's landlady, who owned the high-end dress shop beneath Piper's apartment, but the spare key was hanging from a rack in her office. One of the police department's tech men had tracked down the email message that had been sent to the TV stations. Both it and the attached video clip had been sent from a stolen smartphone. The owner hadn't even noticed it was missing.

The uniformed officers had questioned shop owners, but the incident had taken place hours before most of them had unlocked their doors. When Nelson had left, he'd taken everyone and everything with him—

crime scene techs, the uniforms, the sheet and the rose petals. Back at the precinct, Nelson and his partner would begin the tedious job of trying to track down where the roses and the sheet and the vellum note paper had been purchased. Tedious work, but it might pay off. They might get a description, even a name.

Duncan had hung around, instead of getting a late start to his golf game, because he did some of his best thinking as he wandered through a deserted crime scene. The quiet, the lack of other people, helped him to see things more clearly. He was frequently called in to consult on cases to do exactly what he was doing now. Lingering, noticing the small details, theorizing. He agreed totally with Piper. It wasn't Patrick Lightman who'd done this. Adrienne was checking on the man's alibi, but there were too many things about the scene that didn't fit into the RPK's M.O.

So who had done it? And why? Those were the key questions any profiler asked.

First, the perpetrator was smart. He'd had to gather data on the Lightman case and on Piper's schedule. And to pull it off as a media event in such a short amount of time, he'd had to have contacts at the local new stations.

No matter what angle Duncan viewed it from, he didn't think it was the work of a copycat who was planning to kill other women in the "style" of the RPK. His gut told him that the "who" was someone who had a personal vendetta against Piper. But whoever was trying to get to her was going to have to go through him.

Duncan wasn't sure when he'd made that decision. Perhaps it had been when he'd been studying the rose petals strewn across the sheet and Abe Monticello had mentioned her name. For just an instant, he'd seen the image of her he'd carried somewhere in his head all these years. He'd seen her lying beneath those petals.

Or perhaps it had been a decision that had been made for him seven years ago, when he'd stood under that stone arch with her. He was Scottish enough that he couldn't ignore the power of legends.

When he made the decision, it was irreversible. And it would lead to complications. While she'd been kneeling next to him studying the little picnic scene, he'd wanted his hands on her. And once he started down that path....

When his cell phone rang, he wasn't surprised to see Reid's number on the caller ID. That meant that the news about Piper had made its way to Scotland. And when there was trouble, Cam always made the first call to Reid, the oldest brother.

"I'm assuming you've got Piper's back," Reid said.

"Yes. I assume that our family in Scotland got the news and contacted you."

Reid laughed. "Sibling jealousy just never completely fades away. If it makes you feel better, no one has contacted me. I'm in France again with the VP and I caught it on the evening news. I thought I'd check with you before I got the call. I knew Piper was living in D.C., but I wasn't aware that she was working for Abe Monticello or that she was working on the RPK case. Your paths didn't cross during the trial, I take it."

"The FBI refused to share anything for that appeal."

"What's going on?"

"Wish I had a better handle on that." Then Duncan gave his brother a condensed version of what had happened and what they knew or theorized so far. While it helped to run through all the essentials again, it increased his sense that Piper could really be in danger.

"Could be it's someone who's unhappy with the fact that she helped to set Lightman free."

"That's a long list, but the police will have to start with Suzanne Macks's family, especially her twin brother, Sid." They'd been through quite a bit already. So if he could find anything that would narrow the list and eliminate them....

"I assume you have a plan," Reid said.

"Working on it."

"If I were you, I'd consider getting her the hell out of Dodge. Working on the vice president's security detail, I don't often have the luxury of doing that when my guy becomes a possible target."

"I'm considering that." The problem was to get Piper to agree.

"I'll leave it in your very capable hands, and I'll call the Scotland group to let them know that you're handling it."

After glancing at his watch, Duncan glanced down the alley, trying to see and think about it the same way the man who was threatening Piper's life had. She'd told Nelson that she ran at the same time every morning. That didn't surprise him. Her route took her past the shops on the street. Turning, he stepped out of the alley and glanced up and down the street. It was bustling now with both cars and pedestrian traffic. At six o'clock, she would have been easy to spot from a variety of locations. A regular routine made a serial killer's work easy.

The perpetrator hadn't had much to carry in, Duncan mused as he turned to walk down the alley and climb the stairs. The sheet, a couple of plastic bags filled with petals and the note. Everything could have been easily tucked into one bag. Maybe a backpack or a shopping bag. He recalled Piper's observation that the sheet had been new with the folds from the original packaging still apparent. She had a good eye for detail.

On the landing he crouched down to examine the lock. Duncan found nothing to contradict Nelson's judgment that it hadn't been tampered with. He took a slim tool out of his pocket, and twenty seconds later he was inside the apartment. Then he pantomimed moving the coffee table aside, shaking out the sheet. Thirty seconds. Adjusting and tucking the edges to replicate a perfect square took two minutes. Scattering the petals ate up another thirty. Tops.

He gave himself another thirty to examine the scene in his mind and thirty after that to make adjustments. Then he backed up to the door, took his cell phone out of his pocket and took a video, first panning the scene, then zooming in on the sheet and the petals.

It took him another minute to prop the ladder-backed chair against the door. Halfway down the stairs, he glanced at his watch. Seven or eight minutes from start to finish. Ten if the guy let nerves slow him down. But nothing else in the apartment had been disturbed. Whoever it was had come for one purpose only. To set up the scene, record it and get it on TV.

Mission accomplished.

Then he remembered the bag or whatever the guy must have used to carry in his props. If it had been a shopping bag, it hadn't been in the apartment. And it wasn't needed anymore.

On a hunch, he stopped by the Dumpster at the end of the alley. Duncan held his breath, ignoring the mix of odors he released as he lifted the lid. A Macy's bag lay right on the top, and inside he found a sales slip and the plastic covering for a single sheet.

Bingo.

He had his phone out, intending to pass the information along to Mike Nelson, when a long dark sedan pulled up to the mouth of the alley and his boss stepped out.

Adrienne Monticello was a tall, slender blonde with long curly hair. Today, she wore it pulled back into a ponytail. She had the same camera-ready good looks as her brother and she knew how to dress to enhance them. Her jacket and slacks were purple, her shoes designer. Gold winked at her ears and on her wrist. Although he knew she was in her mid-fifties, she could pass for a decade younger.

She whipped her oversize sunglasses off as she approached, and her expression was worried. "You aren't answering your phone."

"I don't like to be interrupted when I walk through a crime scene." And that's how she'd figured out where to track him down. The fact that she'd left the office to do so didn't bode well.

"Abe called me. He says you don't believe that Lightman was involved in this."

"He wasn't."

She studied him for a moment, and then nodded. "He's worried about Ms. MacPherson. He's been watching the TV coverage at his office, and they've located a photo of her from law school. They're running it along with the little petal scene."

"And Abe noticed that she's the Rose Petal Killer's type. Slender, long brown hair," Duncan added. Serial killers often had a type. Some even went for females who were left-handed or played a certain sport in high school. There'd been one who'd even chosen his victims because of the number and sequence of vowels in their first and last names.

"It isn't just Abe who's noticed it. The press is announcing it to the world about every fifteen minutes or so."

Not good, Duncan thought. That put an even bigger target on Piper's back. One that might tickle the fancy of Patrick Lightman. "Where is she right now?"

"In Abe's offices. He wants protection for her."

What he wanted, Duncan suspected, was for his big sister to help him out of the mess he'd created when he'd ignored her advice and taken the Lightman case.

"I thought you might have some ideas," she said. "Piper MacPherson is your stepsister, right?"

"Yes," Duncan said. "My mother married her father seven years ago, but we've never shared a home." And his feelings for her were definitely not brotherly. "You're having Lightman watched. Does he have an alibi?"

She nodded. "They didn't see him leave his apartment."

"I'm betting there's someone else who has a beef with Piper." He told her about the Macy's bag and the rest of what he was thinking. "It could be Sid Macks, Suzanne's brother." The young man had appeared on all the talk shows he could get himself booked on to protest the release of Lightman and the miscarriage of justice.

"Yeah. He confronted Abe a couple of times outside his office, but he never made any personal threats. He didn't seem the violent type."

"Maybe he or someone else is doing this to get Lightman's attention focused on Piper, hoping he'll do the dirty work."

"Shit. You're making me remember why I hired you. You can really get into the twisted way someone like Lightman would think." She glanced up at the apartment building. "Maybe it's a onetime thing. And maybe you're being paranoid about Lightman. He should be grateful that she helped get him off of death row."

"Hard to bank on that with a crazy psychopath."

"Hannibal Lecter had a soft spot in his heart for Clarice."

"Lecter was a fictional character. Lightman's not. But I may have a plan to keep her out of harm's way for a while." Duncan supposed it had been forming in his mind from the moment she'd walked into her apartment that morning.

"Then it was worth tracking you down in an alley," Adrienne said.

"The problem will be selling it to her."

Adrienne smiled at him. "I can't imagine the day when you won't be able to sell something to a woman."

AT A FEW MINUTES PAST SIX THAT evening, Piper started down the back stairwell in the building where Abe Monticello rented office space. She was wearing dark glasses, and she'd tucked her hair into an old golf cap her boss had dug out of one of his desk drawers.

A disguise.

Abe and Richard were, at this very moment, exiting through the front of the building, thus distracting the few die-hard reporters who had hung out all day hoping to interview her about the Rose Petal Killer's visit to her apartment.

No use telling the media that it hadn't been the real RPK who'd broken into her home and strewn those flower petals around. Some official spokesperson from the D.C. police department had already tried to clarify what had happened. And although the clips had aired all day on the twenty-four-hour cable news stations, first impressions were lasting. And whoever had taken that original video clip and released it to the press had created a dilly of a first impression.

Within hours some enterprising reporter had located her graduation photo from Georgetown Law and she'd become the celebrity of the moment, the latest face that could be blamed for letting Patrick Lightman out of jail.

Duncan had said that she had a target on her back. And by the end of the day, she'd felt it grow brighter and heavier by the moment. It hadn't helped one bit that every time she thought about the target, she thought about him and what she'd imagined doing to him and with him on that sheet in her apartment.

Seeing him again had blown open a floodgate of feelings that she'd successfully buried for years. The intense attraction she'd felt for him at their parents' wedding should have been history.

Piper started down the last flight of stairs. All day she'd tried to convince herself that what she'd felt when she'd seen him that morning had been a fluke. A one-time phenomenon that had been caused by the adrenaline rush of coming home to that terrible scene in her apartment.

But try as she might, she couldn't seem to get Duncan Sutherland completely out of her mind. Even as a child, she'd liked him the best of the triplets. He'd helped her out of an embarrassing situation once. She could still remember it as if it were yesterday. They'd been playing pirates, and Nell had drawn the short straw, which meant that she had to play the captured princess and sit in those dumb caves in the cliff face for hours on end until someone rescued her. Boring. But even though Reid had offered his help, Nell had looked frightened at the prospect of climbing up the cliff face to get to the cave. So Piper had volunteered to take her place.

She'd gotten there just fine because she and Cam, who'd been the pirate that day, had climbed up from the beach. For a while she'd amused herself by poking around in the small string of caves, three of them in total, but after a couple of hours, she'd known them like the back of her hand. Bored out of her mind, she'd decided to rescue herself. But when she'd started down the cliff face, she'd frozen.

When Duncan had arrived to "rescue" her, he'd found her just below the cave, clinging to the rocks. He'd told her he'd be right up, and when he was beside her, he simply told her that he'd go first and tell her what to do.

And he'd done just that, coaching her through it, telling her where to put her hands and feet. He had to have sensed her fear, but he'd never mentioned it or teased her. More importantly, he'd never ratted her out to his brothers or her sisters.

Duncan Sutherland was a man who could be trusted. She only wished she could trust her boss as unconditionally. But something was stopping her. Frowning, she strode down the hallway that led to the alley door. At five o'clock, Abe had called her into his office for a little heart-to-heart talk. He was worried about her safety. There might be other incidents.

Then he'd given her the really bad news.

He wanted her to take some time off. Maybe take a trip just until the media found something else to focus on. When she'd objected and pointed out that she was sitting second chair for the Bronwell trial in two weeks, he'd told her that he'd had to reconsider that decision. Richard Starkweather was going to take her place.

Her already much less than perfect day had become a whole lot worse.

Not that she could fault the logic of Abe's argument. The media circus that had surrounded him right after Lightman had been released had begun to die down. And the break-in at her apartment had stirred everything up again.

Just as seeing Duncan Sutherland had stirred her up again.

No. She was not going to think about him. What she'd felt had been a fluke.

She had bigger problems, not the least of which was the implied death threat on the vellum notepaper. Thus, her Greta Garbo-like exit down the back staircase. Her ride home, arranged by Abe, would be waiting at the end of the alley. And maybe, just maybe, her improvised disguise would allow her to sneak into her apartment unnoticed.

She turned the knob on the alley door. A relaxing bath, layered with bubbles and accompanied by a glass of icy white wine, would help her to think. There'd be other trials. And other setbacks. Piper MacPherson didn't believe that getting depressed or discouraged was ever an effective way to handle life's rough patches.

She was never going to become her father's daughter. He'd avoided life for years after her mother had died. She believed in facing life head-on. She'd figure out a way to deal with the rose petal incident and she'd win back the opportunity to sit second chair with Abe.

The instant she stepped out of the building into the

alley, she stopped short and every thought or plan she had in her mind disappeared. All she could do once again was stare.

Duncan stood leaning against the hood of a very shiny red convertible. The kind that was meant for the open road and speed. Not at all the kind of car she'd expected the quiet, studious Duncan Sutherland to drive.

Neither of those adjectives seemed to apply to the man leaning against the sexy car. He looked as big as he had in her apartment that morning. And his effect on her senses was just as intense. She could see more of him now. A lot more. Broad shoulders tapered down to a narrow waist and then long, long legs crossed at the ankles. With each passing second, the sizzle in her blood grew stronger, hotter.

He'd changed into a black T-shirt and jeans that made him look just a bit dangerous. His face, with its slash of cheekbones, broad forehead, unruly hair and strong chin, was nearly movie star perfect. That was the image of him that had kept sneaking into her mind all day, even when she'd been talking to Abe and losing her dream assignment.

When she met Duncan's eyes, they had the same effect on her senses they'd had that morning, sending a shot of heat that hit her dead center, then radiated right out to her fingers and toes. Okay. The way she was reacting to him was not a fluke and not the result of an adrenaline rush.

Terrific.

As if she hadn't had enough to deal with today. A nut who wanted to scare her, a boss who wanted to protect her, not to mention himself, and now this.

It was only then she realized she wasn't moving.

It was the second time today Duncan Sutherland had stopped her cold.

Time to put an end to that. She'd talk to him and send him on his way. Striding forward, she forced a smile. "We've got to stop meeting like this."

Duncan threw back his head and laughed. Her straightforward, no-nonsense approach was one of the things he'd always liked about Piper. And he was grateful for it now since it had effectively brought him back to the present. For a moment after she'd stepped out of that alley door, she'd wiped his mind clean.

"What are you doing here?" Piper asked as she reached the hood of his car.

He had to think for a second. Looking at her was slowing his thought processes down. But the reason was the same one that had brought him to her apartment that morning. "Your boss called my boss and asked for a favor."

Her brows shot up. "Favor? What kind of a favor? And why would your boss owe Abe Monticello a favor?"

"Family thing. My boss is Adrienne Monticello. She's Abe's younger sister. I suspect she grew up trying to get him out of trouble, and old habits die hard. They're both worried about you."

Duncan watched her absorb the information. While he absorbed more of her. The pantsuit was a pale gray linen with a slim fit that tapered down to narrow ankles and killer heels. When he slowly swept his gaze back up to her face, he saw by her frown that she didn't like his answer, but she got it.

"You're my ride back to my apartment."

"Yes." For starters. He wouldn't tell her his entire plan, not while they were standing in an alley and they hadn't yet discovered who'd set that nasty little scene that morning.

She shifted her gaze to the car and ran her hand over the hood. "Nice ride."

"Nice disguise."

"I had to improvise." She tipped her sunglasses down as she met his eyes. Duncan took the hit dead center and he struggled to keep his thoughts from scattering again. When she pulled the cap off and a rich cascade of dark brown hair tumbled out, he gave up on thinking of anything but the way the sun showered over her long, loose curls, lightening some strands, darkening others. He reached out and wound one of those curls around his finger. He couldn't be sure who had moved, but they were close enough that their fingers had suddenly tangled on the hood of his car. Close enough that he could see a ring of lighter gold surrounding the deep, rich amber shade of her eyes. And he could smell her. Spring flowers—he hadn't forgotten the scent.

If he lowered his head, he could finally taste her. Something he'd been wondering about all day. No. Longer than that. He'd been wondering about her taste for seven years.

Piper's mind was racing almost as fast as her heart but she couldn't seem to latch onto a coherent thought. When she'd started toward him, she'd had a plan. She was going to handle the Duncan problem by politely accepting his ride home and then sending him on his way. And now her fingers were linked with his and the heat from that flesh-to-flesh contact was zinging through her blood.

She could try to blame it on the car. If she hadn't run her hand over the hood, she wouldn't have gotten this close. But a good defense attorney would tear that excuse to shreds and claim she'd put her hand on the hood because she'd wanted this to happen—that she'd been thinking of touching him ever since she'd seen him in her apartment that morning.

Guilty, she thought. And, dammit, now that his mouth was only inches from hers, she wanted to taste him, too.

No. She had to think.

Breathe. The air she gulped in burned her lungs.

Say something. But the desire she was feeling was so huge, so consuming, she couldn't get any words past the dryness in her throat.

They touched nowhere else except where their fingers were linked, but he might as well have been touching her everywhere. And she wanted him to so badly.

With whatever brain cells she had left, Piper figured she had two options. Run or do what she really, really wanted to do. And why not? It had taken a Pandora to open that box and an Eve to sample that apple. Maybe she just needed to know how big a problem she was dealing with. A good attorney built her best cases once she'd read through the discovery. Gripping his shirt with her free hand, she rose on her toes and pulled his mouth to hers.

She might have made the first move, but once she had, Duncan Sutherland was no slouch in the kissing department. The scrape of his teeth had her gasping, then moaning as his tongue seduced hers. Those hands, quick and clever, were everywhere, enticing, exciting. She couldn't get her breath, didn't care if she ever did.

She thought she'd known what to expect.

The jolt was no surprise. But how could she have

known it would knock her off her feet? Or had he
lifted her?

The heat, too, she'd been prepared for. When a man
could make your blood sizzle with a look, heat was a
given. But she hadn't imagined it would have the power
of a blast furnace. Or trigger a need to crawl right into
him until she dissolved.

Excitement was too tame a word for what was
pounding in her blood.

Greed didn't even come close to describing the desperate hunger she was feeling or the urgent need to
satisfy it.

Here. Now.

Had she said the words out loud?

Had he?

ALL DUNCAN KNEW WAS THAT HE couldn't think. She
flooded his senses, blocking out everything else with
her taste, her textures, her scents. He couldn't separate
them. Couldn't possibly name them all. Couldn't resist
taking more, asking for more.

When she wrapped her arms and legs around him,
as much demand as invitation, he was helpless to do
anything other than take them both deeper. No other
woman had ever made him feel helpless. Now she was
taking him places he'd never been before, making him
feel things he'd never felt before.

And why had he waited so long to let her do it?

Here. Now.

The idea of laying her on the hood of his car and
quenching the desire, the need that had gone from
flame to inferno in seconds, flashed brilliantly into
his mind. He wanted, wildly wanted to turn the image
in his mind into reality.

Here. Now.

But he couldn't. With the words still thrumming in his mind and pounding in his blood, he reached deep for control and found it. Easing away, he settled her against the car's fender before he stepped back. His pulse was still racing. His heart slammed like a hammer against an anvil in his chest. And he still wanted her. He had to figure that wasn't going to stop any time soon.

So he had a problem. An even bigger one than he'd anticipated. "That isn't what I came here to do."

"Ditto." She'd folded her arms across her chest, but she was no longer using the car for support. When he noticed he still was, he stepped away.

"We have to figure out a solution to this," she said.

"Agreed."

"I have to think."

Duncan thought the time for that had passed.

"So." She walked around to the passenger door and opened it. "You can take me to my apartment, see that I'm safely locked in and then go away."

Duncan slid behind the wheel and then drove them out of the alley into D.C. traffic. He could go along with one out of three of her directives. But he figured he'd have a better chance of making his case in her apartment.

4

PIPER STOOD IN HER KITCHEN watching Duncan open a bottle of red zinfandel. He'd picked it up with the pizza on the drive back to her apartment.

"We have to talk. You have to eat," he'd said by way of explanation.

She couldn't argue with either point. And she figured she needed to save up her energy. If she was going to argue with Duncan about anything, it was going to be about what she was sure he wanted to "talk" about.

The mind-blowing kiss they'd indulged in.

In an alley. A very public place.

She'd made the move, but at least they knew what they were up against. And she hadn't been the one to call a halt to it. She'd always been able to before. That aside, they had to find a solution. They both worked in D.C. They were adults. And they wanted each other like gangbusters. No way they could ignore the elephant in the room.

She made her living arguing cases, negotiating solutions, and if she'd learned anything from law school and from working for Abe, it was the value of a pre-emptive strike.

So while they'd driven home, she'd tried to review her options. But it was damn hard to weigh them objectively while they'd sat so close in that tiny car. Every time he'd shifted gears, his arm had brushed against hers, and each time it had, "here" and "now" had blinked on and off, little neon letters in her mind.

Now he filled all the spare space in her kitchen. She could even smell him above the spicy aroma of the food.

He'd given her no chance to send him away as he'd cut a path through the little throng of reporters that had been waiting at the mouth of the alley. And she had to admit that she was happy not to have had to enter her apartment alone tonight.

He poured the dark red wine into two glasses and handed her one. "I have a proposition for you."

"Ditto," she said. She just had to figure out what it was. Exactly.

"Mind if I go first?"

"Go ahead." The only thing better than making a preemptive strike was learning what your opponent had in mind and then adjusting your strategy.

"Cam has been bugging me to take a few days off and go up to the castle to see what I can figure out about the rest of Eleanor Campbell MacPherson's missing dowry and about that intruder he believes was breaking into the library. I want you to come with me."

Surprised, Piper stared at him, her mind racing. Duncan Sutherland knew a bit about making preemptive strikes himself, it seemed. "Why would I want to do that?"

He sipped his wine, and then smiled at her. "Be-

cause your sister Adair already found one of the earrings. Don't you want to see what you can do if you
set your mind to it?"

She tilted her head to one side to study him. "My
sisters and I aren't much motivated by sibling rivalry.
And I have a lot on my plate right now."

"Agreed." He finessed two slices of pizza out of the
steaming box and handed her one on a plate. When
they were both seated at the small table, he continued.
"Look, I know that Monticello wants you to keep a
low profile for a while. Part of that is because he is
what he is. He doesn't want the spotlight focused on
anyone else but him. But part of that is motivated by
genuine concern for your safety. He's worried about
you. And what happened today—you can't take that
lightly. My boss isn't taking it lightly. What argument
could I make that would convince you to come up to
the castle with me for a while?"

Piper lifted her glass and swirled the contents. She
took a careful sip before meeting his eyes. "Not a one.
I don't believe in running away from problems."

Okay, Duncan thought. He'd struck out on his
first and second strategies. The missing sapphires
and the safety factor. It struck him quite forcibly that
he didn't know as much as he needed to know about
Piper MacPherson. Therefore, he'd used the wrong ap-
proaches so far. A first for him and totally due to the
fact that for the last seven years he'd tried to avoid
thinking about her, period.

So he did what he'd avoided doing for seven years.
Biting into a slice of pizza, he put himself in her shoes,
the same technique he used on the cases he profiled.
She was tired. There were dark circles under her eyes
and a little worry line on her forehead. The worry line

struck a chord in his memory. When they'd played together as children, she'd always been the worrier about one or the other of her sisters. Protective, too.

And today of all days, why wouldn't she be tired? She'd been instrumental in writing a brief that had let a convicted murderer go free. Monticello's personal hunger for media attention had protected her so far, but now she was suddenly being credited with putting Patrick Lightman on the streets. And someone didn't like that at all.

She didn't like it, either. He'd seen both guilt and regret in her eyes that morning when Abe had been bragging about her brilliant brief. He'd recognized it at the time, but there'd been other things on his mind, including handling his response to her.

He took another sip of his wine. There had to be a better way to convince her.

As silence stretched between them, Piper picked a piece of pepperoni off of her slice and ate it. "Abe is so concerned about my safety that he replaced me as second chair on the Bronwell trial."

"That sucks." The case had made all the papers and hit the national news nearly a year ago. Alicia Bronwell, the trophy wife of one of D.C.'s most highly paid lobbyists, had been accused of slowly killing her much older husband with arsenic. When Abe snatched away Piper's opportunity to participate in the trial, that had to have been a blow. On a day when she'd already sustained a pretty good one.

But it didn't escape him that the loss of the Bronwell trial was foremost in Piper's mind—not the fact that someone might be intending to harm her. The woman had courage. He'd noticed it when they'd been children. There'd been one day in particular when they'd been playing a pirate game on the cliffs. Duncan recalled finding her clinging to the rocks, frozen with fear. She'd climbed down to the beach with him—in spite of the fact that she'd been scared stiff.

She selected a slice of green pepper.

"Monticello offered you second chair as your reward for the work you did on the Lightman case."

When she met his eyes, he saw the anger. "Yes. Then he took it away and gave it to Richard."

Duncan's eyes narrowed. "The guy who barged in here this morning."

"Yes. And he'll take full advantage of the opportunity. Richard's good at that."

"You've had a hell of a day. First a nutcase who wants to annoy and scare you at the very least and, worst case scenario, wants you dead. Then your boss reneges on his offer."

"If you're trying to cheer me up, you're failing."

"I'm not here to cheer you up. I'm just laying a foundation for the case I'm going to make. Isn't that what you'd do with a jury?"

She lifted her glass and studied him over the rim. There was a challenge in her eyes, and they didn't appear as tired anymore. "Go for it, Sutherland."

"Seems to me you have two choices." Holding up a finger, he talked around another bite of pizza. "You can stay here in D.C., deal with the press and hide away in your boss's office while you wait for the guy who staged the scene this morning to make his next move."

She sipped her wine and waited for him to continue.

"That *is* your current plan, right?"

"Close enough."

His eyes narrowed suddenly. "Don't tell me you're

going to try to find out who set up the little scene this morning."

Her eyes widened full of innocence. "Okay, I won't tell you that."

He grinned at her and had the pleasure of seeing surprise flicker over her features. "It's exactly what I would do. But I have a better proposition for you."

The second he saw the pulse flutter at her throat and the color of her eyes darken, Duncan knew he'd chosen the wrong word. *Proposition* had other connotations, and they were both now thinking about the possibilities. They were alone. And it would be so easy to just propose that they finish what they'd started in that alley. Better still, he could shove the pizza aside, pluck her out of that chair and do what he'd wanted to do since they'd walked into her apartment.

Except that wasn't what he was making a case for right now.

"Why don't you help me put Patrick Lightman back in jail?"

She narrowed her eyes, studying him. "Why do I have to go to the castle to do that?"

"Because I'm having all the FBI's files on him delivered up there. My current assignment at work is to review all of the RPK cases and find something that will allow us to charge Lightman again. Cam has been bugging me to go up there and get a feel for the intruder who may come back. So my proposition is— come with me to the castle and help me find what I need in the files."

"Are you serious?"

"I am. I can work there just as easily as I can work in my office at Quantico. My boss thinks it's a great idea, and your boss will be happy if you're safe and out of the public eye for a bit."

She frowned at him. "You've put a sugar coating on it, but it sounds like you want to whisk me off to the castle so that you can babysit me."

He met her eyes very steadily. "I don't think that you can afford to take what happened this morning lightly. To pull off what he did, he had to have stalked you. And I don't think he's through yet."

"Scaring me is not going to work."

"You've made that clear." He selected another slice of pizza, and leaning back in his chair, stretched out his legs. They nearly reached the back of the couch. "You know this place reminds me of a dollhouse." He chewed a bite of his slice, then said, "And you eat like a doll. Don't you like pizza?"

She picked off a mushroom and popped it into her mouth. "I love pizza. But when I'm playing the role of jury I like to give the argument my full attention."

"Okay, scaring you is the stick part of my strategy. The carrot part is that I really want you to work with me on the RPK files. You found things in the trial transcript and in the case files that got Lightman off. That means you have a damn good eye. I saw the proof of that right here this morning. Thanks to you, I think I found the bag the guy used to carry in a brand-new sheet from Macy's." He elaborated on the search Nelson was doing. "I could really use your help. There's something in one of the cases that I'm missing. And I want Lightman back in a cell."

So did she. "I'm not ashamed of the work I did on the case."

"I wouldn't be either. Under all the bombast and drama, Abe Monticello serves an important function in the justice system, and in the end all of us will be safer. You did your job and you did it well."

He could make her feel so many things. The approval in his tone triggered warmth that intensified when their fingers linked again. She felt the pull, the same one she'd felt when their hands had connected on the hood of his car. Her gaze shifted to his mouth, and she felt the pull even stronger than before. They were alone. All she had to do was lean across the table, close the small distance between them, and she could feel more—more than anyone had ever made her feel. And there was more that he could make her feel.

Here. Now. She simply couldn't prevent those words from coming to mind every time he was this close.

"There's a connection between us," Duncan murmured.

There was definitely something between them. She glanced down at their joined hands. She could try to pull her hand away. She might be able to. She might not. He might let her, but he might not. Each possibility brought a separate thrill.

Here. Now.

She met his eyes and saw that he was thinking the same thing. All one of them had to do was make that small move. But she saw something else she recognized, because it matched exactly what she was feeling. Wariness.

Watching each other, they drew their hands back at the same time.

Duncan closed his fingers around his wineglass. "If you agree to come to the castle with me, we can explore the connection. Or not. No pressure. That part's up to you. Bottom line, I'd really like your help."

Piper was surprised that her hand didn't tremble

when she used it to lift her glass. She needed a sip of wine because her throat had gone dry as dust. He was going to leave whatever was going on between them up to her?

Maybe. She wasn't sure she entirely trusted him on that score. As far as no pressure went…there was pressure each time she looked at him.

Duncan leaned forward. "I've never made a case to a jury before. What's the verdict? Will you go with me to the castle?"

She had her mouth open, ready to answer when footsteps pounded on the staircase outside. Duncan was already at the door when someone knocked.

When he opened it, all she could see beyond Duncan's large frame was the face of her visitor, and she recognized it immediately. "Mr. Findley." She crossed to the door. "Duncan, this is Mr. Findley. He runs the coffee shop across the street."

"A deliveryman left these with me earlier today. I promised I would bring them up when you got home. But I wanted to wait until the reporters finally gave up and went away."

"Thanks." But it wasn't until Duncan turned that she saw roses. They were bright red and arranged in a glass vase. Fear knotted in her stomach.

Mr. Findley was already retreating down the stairs as Duncan closed the door.

"Those are not from the RPK," Piper said. "They're from whoever set up that little scene this morning. And he's beginning to annoy the hell out of me."

Duncan took a vellum card out of an envelope and held it out to her.

THE NEXT TIME YOU'LL BE THE ONE LYING BENEATH THE PETALS. THESE PERHAPS.

"The person who sent this note could be just as dangerous," Duncan said.

"I don't want to run away from this. I want to catch him and make him pay."

Duncan set the flowers down, then turned to face her. The anger she saw in his eyes was such a close match to her own that some of her tension eased.

"We're going to catch him," he said. "He's already making mistakes. He left behind that Macy's bag, and he used a florist for this. Mike Nelson will check it out. In the meantime, why not play with his mind the way he's trying to play with yours?" he asked. "Just think of what he'll feel like if you're not here to get the next message or flower delivery. If you come away with me to the castle, it's going to annoy the hell out of *him*."

She studied him for a moment, but the decision had been made. "You're damn good at making a case, Sutherland. I'll pack a bag."

AT FIRST PIPER WASN'T SURE what had awakened her. Not Donald Duck, a fact she discovered when her hand whacked the flat top of the nightstand. And she couldn't see a thing. The lights from the street always filtered in through her bedroom curtains.

By the time her mind had slogged its way through the missing alarm clock and the pitch blackness that surrounded her, lightning flashed outside and the brief illumination chased away her disorientation.

She was in her bedroom at Castle MacPherson. Thunder rumbled. Rain splatted.

Ah, the sounds of home, she thought. Turning on her side, she angled her head toward the windows so that she could see the lightning sparkle and dance across the sky. Nature's fireworks.

For better or worse, she'd let Duncan talk her into
coming here. And he hadn't wasted any time doing it.
He'd called Aunt Vi to let her know they were coming,
and his suitcase and golf clubs had already been in the
trunk of his car when he'd finessed her suitcase in between them. Either he'd been very confident that he'd
be able to talk her into going with him or he'd been prepared to leave without her. She suspected the former.

And she couldn't fault the argument he'd made. Or
the bait he'd used. Offering the opportunity to put Patrick Lightman back behind bars had been the perfect
lure. He had to have known she would jump at it. She
suspected that he was very good at his job.

But if Duncan Sutherland thought he was going to
have everything his way every time, he would be in
for a surprise.

The rain was pouring down now, the thunder crash-
ing overhead. The details of their exit from D.C., while
pushing the speed limit through a series of small towns
in Pennsylvania and New York, were coming back.
Duncan had kept the music loud and tuned to a sta-
tion that played and replayed the top twenty. The fact
that only a few of the songs were familiar to her told
her that she'd been working too hard. It had been after
midnight when they'd reached the castle, but Aunt Vi
had greeted them at the door and hustled them off to
waiting beds.

She'd slept like a rock until now. Nearly 5:00 a.m.
according to the illuminated dial on her watch. Throwing the covers off, she crossed to the sliding doors that
led to one of the castle's many balconies and opened
them. The rain was growing softer already and the
lightning had dimmed to erratic flickers in the slowly
graying sky. Even as a child, she'd loved the storms

that rushed in over the mountain lakes, unleashed their fury, and then blew away. They seldom lasted long.

But then, few things in life did. Everything was temporary. The important thing was to live in the present the best way you knew how. And Duncan had given her the opportunity to do that on a couple of levels. She enjoyed solving problems, the planning, the execution, even the point at which you claimed success and then could put them behind you. For years now, she'd structured her life around projects. Finish college, get into Georgetown Law, make law review. Since she'd worked for Abe, it had been one case after another.

This was the first break she'd had in a long time. Not that it was a break, really. She had two projects to work on. Find something that would put Patrick Lightman back in jail, and decide what to do about the intense, almost primitive attraction she and Duncan were feeling for each other.

She knew what she wanted to do about Duncan. And every time she got near him, she wanted to do it on the spot. No other man had ever tempted her that much or that urgently. But keeping her heart unentangled and fancy-free had been part of her game plan from the time she'd first noticed that boys weren't so scruffy and annoying. During her college and law school years, she'd enjoyed a few relationships with men, but she'd never let them intrude on the rest of her life. If she and Duncan—what was the word he'd used? *Explored*— that was it. If they decided to explore what they were feeling, things were bound to get messy. Not only was there the family angle, but an attraction as consuming as the one she and Duncan were feeling might not be easily corked in a bottle.

Placing her palms on the balcony railing, she stared

out over the garden as the sky slowly lightened. In the
distance, she could see the dark gleam of the lake, quiet
now and smooth, and she could see the stone arch. Two
floodlights had been installed as part of the tightened
security on the castle after a man going by the name of
Nathan MacDonald had planted a bomb behind some
stones in the arch.

Of course, she and her sisters had buried something
very different there—a metal box that contained their
goals and dreams. Piper grinned at the memory. It had
been years since she'd even thought of the box that their
mother had once kept her jewelry in.

When they were just kids, it had been Adair's idea
to write out their goals and dreams on slips of paper,
put them in the box, and by burying it behind loose
stones in the arch, tap into the power of the legend.

Piper's addition to the scheme was that they each
use different colored paper to ensure privacy. Then
Nell had assigned the colors—yellow for Adair, blue
for Piper and pink for Nell. For years they'd made a
habit of sneaking out of the house late at night, digging
up that box and slipping in new goals. The last time
they'd done it had been on the night that their father
had married Beth Sutherland.

Something stirred at the edges of her mind. If she
hadn't thought of the box in years, she certainly hadn't
thought of that night. But little flashes were coming
back to her now. She and Nell and Adair had snuck out
of the castle close to midnight with a bottle of champagne and pads of their appropriately colored paper.
They'd raced a storm to the stones—and won. They'd
toasted their success and their father's wedding with
the champagne, and then at Adair's suggestion, they'd

all agreed to write down an erotic encounter involving their ideal fantasy man.

That part she remembered. But with all the champagne she'd drunk that night and the fact that she'd buried the memory for so long, the details of her fantasy were fuzzy. She knew one thing. It had been the first and only time she'd ever written anything about a man and buried it in the stones. She felt a little stir of unease.

Hours earlier on that same day, she'd met Duncan's eyes beneath those stones and she'd felt things she'd never experienced before. Had she been thinking of him when she'd written out her fantasy? Turning, she paced into her room. He'd certainly been on her mind that day. But she'd managed to avoid him. And he and his brothers had left to fly back to their respective colleges shortly after the ceremony. So she probably would have thought of anyone *but* him when she was composing her erotic fantasy.

Or she might have been thinking *only* of him. A mix of emotions moved through her—anticipation, excitement, panic. Lots of the other goals she'd tucked into that box had become a reality—starting with the medals she'd won in her elementary school's yearly spelling bee and right up to and including her law degree at Georgetown.

Before she decided exactly what she and Duncan would *explore,* it would be good to know what she was dealing with. Discovery was essential before you built a case for trial. Gathering all the facts was equally important in making any intelligent decision. Ignorance could come back and bite you hard.

And there was no time like the present to find out exactly what her fantasy had been all those years ago. Turning back into her room, she found sweats and shoes in her suitcase and pulled them on. For a second, she thought of running down the stairs to the foyer and disarming the security system Vi had shown them.

But there was a quicker way to the stone arch. She wasn't enamored of heights, especially if she had to climb down instead of up. But after the summer when the Sutherland boys had been focused on playing pirates on the cliffs and she'd discovered her fear, she'd worked on it by frequently climbing down to the garden from her balcony. Of course, her sisters had been with her then to silently cheer her on. And it had been a while since she'd practiced…

Her stomach took one, queasy roll as she threw her leg over the railing. Then she used the thick vines covering the stones to climb down. By the time she reached the ground, she was breathing hard and grinning in triumph. Then, in the growing morning light, she raced to the stone arch to find the metal box she and her sisters had buried their dreams and fantasies in.

5

As Piper reached the clearing, the eastern sky was lightening and just the rim of a red sun could be seen peeking out over the tips of the pines across the lake. The stone arch that Angus—Eleanor Campbell MacPherson's husband—had built lay at the far end of the garden. It was about ten feet long, eight feet or so wide and the ceiling arched to about ten feet. The fact that it had stood for more than two centuries testified to her several-times-great grandfather's engineering and construction skills. It had even withstood a lightning strike about a month ago.

It didn't take Piper long to find the box. The stones that concealed it in the niche were loose, as if they'd recently been replaced. By Adair, no doubt. Her older sister had been living here at the castle for more than six months. It was a good possibility she'd dug up the secret container they'd stored their fantasies and dreams in. It was about the size of a cigar box, made of metal, and it had a little padlock about as secure as one that came on a young girl's diary.

In fact, it had, if she remembered correctly. One of

Adair's. After wiggling the box out of its niche, she sat down on the flat rocks that formed the base of the stone arch and placed it in her lap. Just looking at it jogged a few more details loose. Nell had wanted to know how erotic their sexual fantasy could be.

"No holds barred." That had been her answer to her baby sister. And she'd been thinking about Duncan when she'd said it. It was coming back to her now. Once they'd exchanged that look while their parents had spoken their vows, she hadn't been able to quite put him out of her mind.

She couldn't put him out of her mind now. The chemistry between them was so strong, so primal. The stuff that sexual fantasies were made of. As she ran her hand over the box, she could have sworn the metal grew warmer. She examined the tiny padlock and saw that it had rusted through, so she removed it.

Lifting the top, she found the contents just as she remembered—three separate compartments, each holding different colored paper. Picking up the folded blue sheets on the top of her pile, she opened them.

The heading read My Fling With My Fantasy Man: Sex on Demand.

She felt her heart skip a beat. Then and now. Those were the words that said it all when she'd imagined the sexual fantasy that she wanted to bring to life with Duncan Sutherland. Oh, she might have buried the memory away, but if anything, it had just grown stronger.

At nineteen, it had described her ideal sexual fantasy period. She'd been in her sophomore year of college, and all her friends had been raving about the benefits of having a friend they could call on for sex on demand. *Buddy sex* was what they'd called it. It was convenient, no fuss and no bother.

Piper skimmed the first page. She'd gone way beyond what her friends had talked about. And like any good prelaw student, she'd defined her terms and embellished them as she'd argued the benefits. Sex on demand with a willing partner was simple, straightforward and didn't require all the time-consuming trappings that went along with dating and romance. It further prevented complications from spilling over into the other more important aspects of your life— like your work, your goals, your dreams.

The "sex on demand"—she was finding that aspect on the page in spades. She recalled just how fast her pen had moved over the blue paper trying to capture all the images she'd had in her head of having sex with him anytime, anyplace and in any position. By the time she'd finished skimming the second page, her heart was racing and her whole body had heated. She'd even written about making love with Duncan in that cave he'd rescued her from.

An image of doing just that flashed brilliantly into her mind. It was followed by another—the two of them standing in the alleyway at the back of Abe's office building. They'd come very close to having on-demand sex right on the hood of her car. Earlier that day, when they'd been in her apartment kneeling together on the floor, she'd imagined having sex with him right on that petal-strewn sheet.

She couldn't seem to look at him without thinking, *here* and *now.*

What if she could have sex on demand with Duncan—no holds barred? The idea thrilled her.

And why not?

She pressed a hand to her heart to make sure it didn't beat its way right out of her chest. Coming up here to the castle with him certainly hadn't been something she'd planned on. But a girl was a fool not to take advantage of the opportunities that life offered.

Then a thought struck her and an alarm bell jingled at the edge of her mind. She shifted her gaze back to the subtitle and skimmed the pages again. Discovery—that's what she'd come here for. And good discovery triggered questions. In this case a couple of very big ones.

The alarm bell went from jingle to clang. What if what she'd written down on these pages was influencing, perhaps even dictating, what she was feeling now for Duncan? What if the stones and the legend were playing some kind of role in making her want Duncan so badly?

She felt panic surge and shoved it down. She'd never solved one problem in her life by panicking. And it wasn't like she'd actually kissed Duncan in the stone arch. All she'd done was lust after him—very imaginatively and in great detail.

You had to actually kiss someone beneath the stone arch before the legend kicked in. She could argue that major distinction to any jury of her peers and win.

And sex on demand with Duncan was perfect as long as it had no strings, no expectations—all the good points her college buddies had raved about with "buddy sex." It would be the perfect arrangement for them while they were here. She could make that case to Duncan. And she couldn't imagine him having a problem with it.

A sound, a bell jingling, had her glancing up and she saw Alba, the dog her aunt had brought home from a shelter, approaching. They'd met briefly when she and Duncan had arrived the night before. If Alba had been sent to find her, that meant that her aunt Vi was up and Duncan might already be up, too.

She folded the sheets of blue paper, carefully tucked them back into the center compartment, then set the now useless padlock back in place. Then she put the fantasy box back where it been for the last seven years. She might not have figured out what she could do about the rest of her problems, but she'd definitely decided what she wanted to do about Duncan Sutherland.

WHEN DUNCAN WALKED INTO THE kitchen, he found himself greeted by the scent of freshly brewed coffee and a warm hug from Viola MacPherson. Now she was his mother's sister-in-law, but he would always remember her as the warm, loving woman who'd baked cookies and applied first aid on that long-ago summer when he and his brothers had spent nearly every day at Castle MacPherson while his mother researched the MacPherson family in the castle's library.

Minutes later, he was seated at the table in the sun-drenched kitchen and she was setting platters of scrambled eggs, bacon and her homemade scones in front of him. Then she poured herself a cup of tea and sat down across from him.

"Shouldn't we wait for Piper?" he asked as she loaded a plate for him and then one for herself.

"You'll starve if you wait for her. Eats like a bird. From the time she was a little girl, she's been a grazer. When she finally comes in from the stone arch, she'll go for coffee first and pick at half a scone. Then she might have a banana."

"She's out at the stone arch?" He was halfway out of his chair when Vi signaled him back down.

"She's safe enough. I sent Alba to her. Our dog may be deaf, but she senses things."

"Cam told me about Alba's talents." His brother's theory about an intruder visiting the castle's library for six months had been largely due to Alba's barking in the middle of the night. But the security on the castle, and especially the library, had been tightened since then. And he'd taken the time to check it out last night.

"She hasn't sensed anyone visiting the library lately, I take it."

Vi shook her head. "Things have been very quiet here since you delivered our last bridegroom and saved the day. No lightning strikes. No bombs. The most exciting thing we have planned all weekend is a photo shoot tomorrow morning."

As he dug into his eggs, Duncan reviewed the theory that Cam had given him, picturing it in his mind—someone sneaking in after everyone had gone to bed, making himself at home in the library and taking his—or her—time to search it thoroughly. It spoke of someone who was very patient. But it also indicated someone who had good reason to believe that he would find what he was looking for. Cam's theory was that the intruder had been searching for the location of Eleanor's sapphires. Then two things had happened. First, Adair had found one missing earring, and for the past month access to the library and the castle had been shut down. Not only had the intruder's easy-come, easy-go nighttime visits been cut off by a new security system, but Cam and Daryl had installed cameras and added laser light technology to the alarm system in the library.

Whoever the intruder was, he couldn't be happy with either development. And he was probably trying to find another way to gain access to the castle and the library. That's what Duncan would do. So there could very well be a storm brewing from that direction.

"How long has Piper been out there?" Duncan asked as he reached for his coffee.

"Probably since first light. Although I hope she got some sleep first." Vi sipped her tea. "From the time they were little, all three of them used to make midnight visits to the stone arch to share secrets, make plans, dream dreams. They even used to write their goals down. They buried them in a box in the stones so that they could tap into what Adair always called the 'power of the stones.' They used to leave from Piper's room because they could easily climb down from her balcony." Vi's smile held a hint of nostalgia. "They didn't think I knew about that part."

"You kept pretty good track of your girls back then," Duncan said. And she still did. When he'd called the castle last night to let Vi know they were coming, she'd already been aware of the incident at Piper's apartment and the resulting media storm. He reached across the table and gave her hand a squeeze. "I'm going to keep her safe. And we're going to find out who's targeting her."

"I know. I talked to Daryl after I spoke with you," Vi said. "He thinks that getting her out of D.C. was a good idea."

The instant she mentioned Daryl's name, a pretty blush rose in Vi's cheeks. Duncan smiled at her. "It's always good to know that the director of the CIA's domestic operations unit thinks I'm on the right track."

Duncan lifted her hand to examine her engagement ring. "Daryl has good taste."

Vi sighed. "It is lovely, isn't it?"

"I was talking about you, but the ring is lovely, too. Have you and Daryl set a date yet?"

"First weekend of September. Adair has already put our names on the wedding schedule. Daryl flew into Albany yesterday on some kind of business, and since I'm attending and presenting at a big wedding fair at one of the malls, I'm going to join him for dinner, and then I'm bringing him back here for the weekend. He wants to be here for that photo shoot tomorrow with *Architectural Digest*. He's looking forward to meeting Piper."

"Is he worried about the shoot?"

"No. Daryl checked out the man who's coming. Russell Arbogast is a senior editor and writer with the magazine. They've been running a series on Scottish castles and they want to include a feature article on the replica Angus One built of his ancestral home. With Cam and Adair both gone, Daryl didn't want me to have to handle it alone."

"It's always good to have the CIA on the premises for backup."

Vi smiled at him. "The only person who might not be a happy camper this weekend is Piper. I can't imagine she's taking well to the idea of being boxed in and… bodyguarded."

Duncan sipped coffee. "I've asked her to help me with a case we both have an interest in. The Rose Petal Killer. We're going to see if there's a way we can put Patrick Lightman back in jail. The files are being delivered this morning."

"How clever of you. It's the perfect project for her. I can see why you're good at your job."

"I also told her about Cam's certainty that the rest of Eleanor's sapphires are somewhere on the estate."

"Daryl and I agree with him on that."

As he speared more bacon, Duncan asked, "Why do you think she buried one of the earrings separately?"

Vi sipped her tea. "You're assuming Eleanor did it?"

"They were hers. And she wore them in her wedding portrait. The fact that there's no record of them after her death argues that she's the one who hid them. Angus died first, so that lets him off the hook unless they hid them together at some point. Cam has my mom researching the Mary Stuart connection, but that photo they reprinted in the *Times* article argues heavily in favor of the tradition that's been handed down about their connection to Mary Stuart. They're worth a fortune now. But even back then, they would have had that added value. If I had something like that, I'd protect it."

"From what?" Vi asked.

He smiled at her. "Good question."

With a smile, she reached over and laid a hand over one of his in a gesture that he remembered from that long-ago summer. "You'll figure it out. That's what you do best."

A chime sounded, followed by muffled knocks on a door.

"That will be Russell Arbogast." Vi rose from her chair and carried her teacup to the sink. "He wanted to bring his photographer here for a tour prior to the shoot tomorrow."

At the kitchen door, Vi turned and waved her hands in a shooing gesture. "Go on out and check on Piper. She's probably fallen asleep. There were mornings when I'd find all three of them sleeping in that stone arch."

Duncan exited through the terrace doors and headed toward the garden path. He heard the jingle of a bell before he spotted Piper on the grass in front of the stone arch. The impact on his senses was instantaneous. Every muscle in his body tightened and hardened; heat flared in his center and then spun outward just as it had yesterday morning when she'd barged into her apartment, and yesterday afternoon when she'd stepped into the alley.

He had no control over the way his body reacted to her. He'd always preferred to have control where women were concerned, and he'd never had a problem before.

She didn't even seem to be aware of him right now. She tossed a stick and then waited for the dog to retrieve it, a game that both dog and woman seemed to be thoroughly enjoying. The jingling bell hung from the dog's neck as a precaution in case she wandered off.

There was a car parked in front of the house, a new black SUV. Aunt Vi's visitors, he assumed. He paused beneath a trellis covered in roses and turned his full attention back to Piper. She wore comfortable-looking sweats and sneakers. Her hair tumbled down over her shoulders. When she tossed the stick, then raced with the dog to get it, her hair flew out behind her like a flag.

It had felt like silk, sliding through his fingers when he'd kissed her, and he wondered just how long he could wait to get his hands in it again. He could cross the distance to her in seconds, he thought. And once he closed that distance and touched her again, he couldn't trust himself to stop.

He'd promised her that she would make the decision.

Not so much because he was generous or thoughtful, but because he was hesitant. Very few things made him feel that way. Oh, he made a practice of sitting back and studying all the angles of a situation before he acted. But once he knew what he wanted, once he saw the answer, he went after it.

He wanted Piper. He'd never wanted anyone as much. So she was unknown territory for him. He'd recognized that much seven years ago. The one thing he was certain of was that they were going to make love. The attraction between them was too intense for either one of them to walk away.

The problem was he couldn't see what lay beyond that. Pursuing a relationship with her would be like plunging off a cliff into a river without knowing what would happen next.

Duncan had always preferred to know.

The ringing of his cell interrupted his thoughts. Pulling it out, he noted the ID. Mike Nelson. A glance at his watch told him that the detective had probably just arrived at his office.

"Good or bad news?" he asked.

"A mixed bag," Mike said. "I checked out Suzanne Macks's family. All of them, including her brother, Sid, have a solid alibi for yesterday morning. He was working the night shift at a pediatric care unit. He left the hospital at seven-thirty. Of course, he could have hired someone, so we'll keep working on that angle. We're still checking Macy's stores. There are a hell of a lot of them in the area. But we've got a date from the sales slip, and someone may recall selling a single sheet like that."

"And?" Duncan prompted. Mike hadn't called him merely to report on progress. Duncan had called him before he and Piper had left her apartment last night to report the delivery of the vase of roses, and they'd left her key taped to the underside of her stair railing.

"I dropped by Ms. MacPherson's apartment on my way into the office."

Not good, Duncan thought. Mike lived in Maryland and a jaunt through Georgetown was not on his way.

"I figured I'd pick up the flower delivery and save a uniformed officer the trip. I got there about the time she'd be going out for her run just in case someone showed up. No one did."

"But…" Duncan prompted again.

"Someone had visited the place before I did, and they left another bouquet of red roses in front of her door."

"Was there a message?"

"'Till next time.'"

Duncan let out a breath he hadn't been aware he was holding. Whoever was after her wasn't letting up.

"I went in to collect the delivery from last night. Different florist shop. But the messages are written in the same block letters. I'll have someone check both stores out today. Thought you'd want to know."

"Thanks, Mike," Duncan said.

"Serve and protect. That's the job description," Mike said with a yawn. "I'll keep you updated. You keep her safe. She's taking a hell of a beating in the press here. Suddenly, she's the new poster girl for setting a serial killer free. Getting her out of town for a bit was a good idea."

Duncan was about to repocket his phone when it rang again. This time it was his boss.

"Adrienne, what's up?"

"Just checking in. I'm assuming you and Ms. MacPherson are together and safe."

"That was my assignment," Duncan said.

"I'm worried. The press coverage she's getting makes her out to be an even bigger villain than my brother. That can bring the crazies out of the closet."

Duncan watched as an overnight delivery service truck appeared in the drive that ended at the castle doors. Piper noticed it also and then seemed to notice him.

As she moved in his direction, he filled Adrienne in on the two flower deliveries.

There were several beats of silence on the other end of the line. He could picture Adrienne in her office pacing. Thinking. He let the beats continue.

"I never asked where you were going. And I don't want to know. Abe has already called me to find out where Piper is in case he needs to ask questions about the Bronwell trial. She hasn't been picking up her cell."

"Tell him to keep trying," Duncan said.

"Tell her to keep a lid on her location. It might have been someone in Abe's office who leaked the information that she was involved in the Lightman brief."

As the deliveryman in the truck walked toward him, Duncan thought of how easy it might be to figure out exactly where he was. And exactly where Piper MacPherson might have sought temporary refuge. "You're worried."

"All the media attention could get Lightman focused on her. Find something that will allow us to put him back in jail."

"Consider it done. I'm taking delivery on the files I shipped as we speak." Duncan moved toward the deliveryman so that he could sign.

"Thanks," Adrienne said.

Duncan repocketed his cell. Adrienne had come to him at her brother's request to get Piper safely out of the way. Now she suspected someone in his office might have played a role in what was happening to her. Did she suspect Abe?

An interesting question, Duncan thought. And one he'd been trained to find the answer to.

He'd also been trained about what to do with regards to his feelings for Piper MacPherson. Considering the danger she was in—the danger she could be in—he should put anything personal on hold. He thought about that as she walked to join him on the driveway, the dog at her heels.

He could keep her safe from whoever had left the sheet and the roses. He wished he could be equally certain about keeping either of them safe from what they were feeling.

6

"WHAT DO YOU THINK, ALBA?" Piper turned in a full circle for the dog's benefit before she faced herself in the mirror again. Alba was sitting at the foot of her bed, her head raised and cocked to one side.

"No comment, huh?" She could hardly blame the dog. All in all, it was a diplomatic response. She just wasn't a femme fatale. And her wardrobe components were sadly lacking. The jeans and Georgetown T-shirt she'd dug out of her suitcase were pretty much the cream of the crop. And the best word she could come up with to describe the outfit was *plain*.

"He didn't give me any time to pack. Plus, I was thinking comfortable clothes for poking around in the library and searching through files. My only salvation is that I do have a weakness for pretty underwear. Wearing boring and conservative 'law suits' can do that to a woman."

Glancing at Alba, she pressed a hand against her stomach to stop the nerves from jittering. She was babbling to a dog who couldn't hear her and taking way too much time to get dressed.

She'd made a decision, hadn't she? If she could find the courage to act on it. She'd already missed one opportunity when Duncan had first come to the edge of the garden. Though she'd continued to toss sticks to Alba, she'd been aware of him in every pore of her body. Her heart had started racing, breaths had been harder to catch, and the image had flashed brilliantly into her mind of just racing to him and jumping him right there beneath the rose trellis. It would have been wild and wonderful and *totally* unlike her.

But so exactly like her fantasy. With a sigh, she sat down on the bed next to the dog. "I have sex-on-demand on the brain all right. But I chickened out."

Instead of making her fantasy a reality, she'd picked up the stick, tossed it in a direction away from Duncan, and then raced Alba to get it.

Oh, she'd made a case for her cowardice. There'd been those two visitors who had arrived in the SUV a short time earlier. One had been dressed like a fashion plate, the other had carried a camera. If either or both were prospective clients, Aunt Vi would no doubt show them around. Piper was pretty sure that the sight of naked people coupling beneath the rose trellis wasn't on the regular tour. And something else had given her pause. When she'd allowed herself to take a quick look at Duncan out of the corner of her eye, she'd seen that she was probably alone in her thoughts about naked coupling. He'd been on his phone.

But then, he hadn't started his day reading a red-hot fantasy with him in the leading role. She had.

The jingle of a bell brought Piper's full attention back to Alba, who had settled her head on her paws and was studying her intently.

"Here's the problem. Duncan and I might not be on

the same wavelength. He seems totally focused on the work he came up here to do."

When she'd finally approached him in the driveway of the castle, he'd invited her to join him in the library and start working on the RPK files after she'd eaten something. Then Duncan had turned his attention back to the deliveryman and the stack of boxes he'd unloaded from his truck.

"Very businesslike. Very FBI. Maybe he's just doing what he said he'd do—letting me make the decision."

Alba merely returned her gaze.

Piper frowned. "Or maybe he's having second thoughts about the whole exploring thing."

Alba remained silent.

She sprang up from the bed and paced a few feet away. "Now *that* I can see. The main reason he wanted me to come up here with him was to keep me out of harm's way." She turned back to face the dog. "All the Sutherlands have this protective streak that runs deep. A kind of inner white knight—rescue-the-damsel-in-distress thing. Only I don't need someone to rescue me. And I don't need someone to back out on a deal."

Alba raised her head, jingling her bell.

"Exactly. I may have some wardrobe problems, but I have the winning argument. Sex on demand. Anytime, anyplace, any way. It's the perfect relationship for us. Win-win." As she spoke, some of the images from her fantasies slipped into her mind, but she pushed them ruthlessly away. It was time to stop thinking about them and make them real.

"I'll just have to make my case. And I'm good at deflating counterarguments. C'mon, girl." She strode to the door and opened it. Then with Alba at her heels, she headed down the hall and started down the stairs.

DUNCAN STOOD JUST INSIDE THE first-floor entrance to the library. But it was not where he wanted to be. He'd been at loose ends ever since he'd watched Piper run up the grand staircase to change her clothes. And he'd checked his watch several times, wondering why she hadn't joined him yet.

Twenty minutes had gone by, but it seemed longer. After he'd sent the deliveryman on his way, he'd fixed a plate of food for Piper to graze on and put it in the library. Then Vi had invited him into the main parlor to meet Russell Arbogast and his photographer Deanna Lewis. Both had seemed fascinated by Eleanor's portrait and the sapphires. Duncan sensed Arbogast had been less than pleased with the news that they wouldn't be allowed access to the library during their photo shoot. But Vi had smoothed over the news by showing them Angus One's secret cupboard.

Cam and Daryl had decided that no one outside the family would be allowed access to the library until they figured out exactly who'd been visiting it secretly. And that particular mystery was part of the reason he'd come to the castle, Duncan reminded himself.

He stifled the urge to look at his watch again. It was time to focus on work.

Closing the door behind him, he stepped farther into the long, narrow room and tried to clear his mind. Once Piper joined him that could be problematic. Intellectually, he might have decided to keep his distance, but when she'd walked up to him in the driveway, he'd had to stuff his hands in his pockets to keep from touching her. Right now, he wanted to go find her.

Ruthlessly, he pushed that thought aside and made himself focus on the library as if it were a crime scene. The room was two stories high with an iron-railed walkway running around the second level of book-shelves. Cam's theory was that after successfully gaining access to the castle, the intruder had entered through the door he'd just closed. The sunlight filtering in through the sliding glass doors that opened to a terrace on this level and a balcony on the floor above didn't do much to penetrate the gloom. In the middle of the night, the intruder would have needed a flashlight—a high-powered one.

As Duncan strode down the length of the room, the scent of dust and leather assaulted his senses. Piper's father had locked the room up after his first wife's death, and the last person who'd made any use of the room had been his mother when she'd done her research that summer nearly two decades ago. Books stuffed the shelves both horizontally and vertically. Others had spilled into piles on the floor. If someone had come here with the intention of finding some clue to the whereabouts of Eleanor's jewels, it would be a formidable task. Even with a small crew of helpers, it would take time to search through all the books on both floors.

But Cam believed it had been one intruder, someone who'd begun that search in a very careful and organized fashion. The only evidence he or she had left behind had been in disturbing the dust on the lower shelves along one wall from the outside terrace doors to well past the fireplace.

Duncan studied the shelved books as he walked back the way he'd come. He noted the way the dust had been disturbed and in some cases cleaned away. Then he walked around the entire perimeter of the room. None of the other shelves looked disturbed, and he estimated that in six months, the intruder had methodically looked through less than one third of the library's collection. Which meant he could have more than a year's work ahead of him.

That argued for both patience and determination. But it also indicated the same kind of obsession that most serial killers had when they stalked their prey. Whoever had paid regular visits to this library wanted those sapphires and they wouldn't give up. Obviously, someone believed that the priceless jewels were still here on the grounds somewhere and that there was some kind of clue—a map or drawings, a diary perhaps, that would reveal the location. Or locations. Maybe they'd even suspected that the sapphires might have been concealed in one of the books. People frequently used books as hiding places. All Eleanor would have had to do was hollow out the center, tuck her dowry inside and place the book on a shelf with all the others.

But she hadn't. Still, she might have hidden a map or a drawing into one of the books. The fact that one of the sapphire earrings had shown up would only fuel the person's determination. Obsession was never good news. In fact, there was a strong possibility that what he was beginning to feel for Piper might be headed down that path.

The question was, did he have any chance of preventing that? An impossible question to answer when he didn't know if he could keep his hands off her once she walked through that door.

Work, he thought as he shifted his gaze to the seven boxes of files that he'd had the deliveryman line up along the wall. The only strategy he had open to him was to keep them both focused on the work they'd come here to do.

PIPER STOPPED ON THE LANDING the second she saw that her aunt Vi was in the foyer, and she wasn't alone. She recognized the couple who'd arrived earlier in the SUV, and she took a minute to study them. The man was tall in his late thirties with sandy-blond hair and handsome, photogenic features. His suit was Italian, she guessed, and probably tailored especially for him. The pretty brunette standing next to him was wearing jeans, a T-shirt and carried a very professional-looking camera.

Alba growled at her side.

Vi glanced up the stairs and made a quick hand signal to the dog that silenced her. Then she smiled. "Piper, you're just in time to meet Mr. Arbogast and Ms. Lewis. They're from *Architectural Digest*. They're doing a feature article on the castle, and they'll be doing a photo shoot tomorrow."

The man smiled up at her, and by the time Piper reached the group, he had his hand already extended. "Russell Arbogast. This place is such a find." His smile was warm as were his eyes, and the slight accent added to his charm. "We've been running a series on Scottish castles, and when we came across the article in the *Times,* we called your sister immediately to book a shoot. I'm so glad we did. The photos they ran don't do it justice. Deanna here will remedy that."

"Yes," the woman said. Her smile was just as warm as Russell's.

Piper might have extended her hand to Deanna, but Russell hadn't let go of it yet. Not that he was holding it captive. His grip was light, the sensation was pleasant. Piper couldn't help but recall how different her reaction had been when her fingers had accidentally tangled with Duncan's on the hood of his car.

"We're going to do the official shoot tomorrow,"

Russell continued. "I like to make a preliminary visit just to get an overview. And Deanna here likes to take candid shots so that she can more efficiently map out the plan for her assistants. Your aunt has given us a tour, and we understand you're here with Mr. Sutherland on a working vacation. Perhaps after Deanna and I get settled in at the Eagle's Nest in Glen Loch, we could set up a time for an interview. I'd love to be able to include some of your memories growing up here in my article."

"I don't see why we can't arrange something," Piper said.

"Good." Russell gave her hand a quick squeeze before he released it. "Good. I'll be in touch."

After closing the front door, Vi turned to her. "They love the castle. I can't wait to tell Adair. She'll be thrilled. She set up the whole thing." Then she glanced at her watch. "Goodness. I have to get started if I'm going to get to Albany in time for my presentation at the bridal fair. Duncan's in the library with those boxes he had delivered. He's turned off the security for the terrace door so that you can work in there."

Vi scooped up a sweater and her purse from a nearby table. "Lock the door after me and key in the alarm when I leave."

Piper found herself doing just that. Then she narrowed her eyes. It wasn't like her aunt to just hurry off like that—without offering her coffee or homemade scones or something. But Vi MacPherson was no dummy. Could be she'd picked up on the attraction that was sizzling in the air between Duncan and her. So she was giving them some privacy.

"Time to put it to good use," she murmured to the dog as she led the way down the hall. When they reached the library door, the dog pattered on past her into the kitchen and Piper watched her stretch out in a patch of sunlight.

Okay, the verdict was unanimous. She and Duncan needed privacy. Hadn't she already decided how to put it to good use? Straightening her shoulders, she opened the door and stepped into the library. Books were everywhere, spilling off the shelves into random piles on the floor. Dust motes fought for space in the shafts of light that poured in through the tall windows and sliders. And she could see Duncan's silhouette at the far end of the room. He was seated at a desk, his back to her. And still she felt the incredible pull on her senses.

She looked at him and she wanted. It was that simple. That primitive. Her throat went dry as dust. And she wasn't even aware that she'd started walking toward him until she passed the fireplace.

"I've lined up the cases my unit has been able to attribute to the RPK," he said without turning.

Piper stopped and glanced at the boxes that were lined up neatly along the wall between the fireplace and where he was sitting.

"I thought I'd start with the most recent. You can start at the beginning and we'll meet somewhere in the middle."

"Good plan," she said. And he'd started without her. The lid on the box closest to his desk was open and he had file folders stacked beside him.

"Vi said you didn't have breakfast so I fixed a plate for you," he said. "You must be hungry."

She was, but not for food. Still, when she glanced over and saw the tray her heart did a funny little bounce. It held a carafe of coffee, two cups, a plate of her aunt's scones with honey and a couple of bananas.

She'd taken care of herself for years, ever since she'd left the castle to go to college. But Duncan wanted to feed her. Pizza and wine last night, bananas and scones this morning. She moved to the table, picked a banana up.

"While you eat, I want to talk to you about us."

The words, the way he'd said them, had her forgetting all about the banana. A replay of the scenes of the morning flashed through her mind. Duncan standing in the driveway telling her to join him when she was dressed. Duncan informing Russell Arbogast that she was here on a working vacation. And now, Duncan providing breakfast and lining up her work for her. Clearly, the plan was to keep their relationship strictly professional.

To hell with that.

And he still wasn't looking at her. She glanced down at the banana and stifled the urge to throw it at him.

"Okay," she said. "Let's talk." They were going to do a lot more than that.

He turned to look at her. She stopped short when she saw he was wearing glasses, and everything inside of her went into a meltdown. They made him look even sexier, which just wasn't fair. She could hear her brain cells clicking off.

"Take those glasses off. They're killing me."

"Killing you?" He took them off and set them carefully on the desk.

Piper felt her knees again. "I have a few things to say to you." At least she had when she'd been talking to Alba. "White knight," she managed.

"White knight?" Duncan swiveled his chair toward her and stretched out his legs. "You're going to have to explain."

Okay, the glasses were gone, but that incredible body was still there. And right now, just looking at him with those long legs and the hands steepled together had her tapping into all of her mental reserves.

She fastened her gaze on his face. "You and your brothers have all inherited the white knight gene. You like to ride to the rescue and save damsels in distress." She paused to point the banana at him. "You don't have to take care of me or feed me. I can take care of myself and I make my own decisions. I agreed to come up here and work with you on the Lightman files and look for those sapphires, but we also agreed on something else. I get to decide if we're going to explore what's... what's happening between us."

He opened his mouth, but she jabbed the banana in his direction again. "I know what you're going to say. I'm in danger, and if we decide to pursue what we started when we kissed in the alley yesterday, we might get distracted. It might be safer and more productive if we just put that all on hold until we can figure out who's sending me flowers and find another part of Eleanor's dowry. Plus we have to find something that will put Lightman back in jail." She waved her free hand at the boxes. "Have I hit the highlights?"

A little uncomfortable and totally fascinated that she'd read him so clearly, Duncan could see why Abe Monticello had hired her. She had a knack for summation that would be a boon to any trial lawyer. Then she stepped fully into one of the shafts of light from the glass behind him, and he became almost as fascinated by the way the sun played up the different colors in her hair.

"Well?" she prompted.

"What?"

"Are you following me?"

He put some effort into gathering his thoughts. "Except for the white knight part, everything you've said has crossed my mind." In fact, the ideas had been spinning on a nonstop carousel ride through his head since she'd crossed the driveway to him that morning. "I'm worried about you." He told her about the phone calls he'd received from Detective Nelson and his boss. "The person who staged that little scene in your apartment is not giving up. I don't want to put any added pressure on you."

"How's this for pressure? I can't stop thinking about getting my hands on you."

"Ditto." And the only way he was preventing himself from doing just that was by clamping them around the arms of his chair.

"Then why are we talking?" She glanced down at the banana she'd been pointing at him and suddenly tossed it over her shoulder. "I'm betting it's a lot more distracting to think about having hot monkey sex than it is to actually have it."

Monkey sex. Duncan's mind took one long spin.

"You said it was going to be my decision. So, I'm proposing that for the time we are here at the castle, we simply offer each other sex on demand."

"Sex on demand?"

"Yes. My college roommates used to rave about their buddy-sex arrangements. Today, I think they call it friends with benefits. We just make sex available to each other whenever we want it. It's perfect for us and our current situation. No strings. No expectations. Anyplace, anytime, any-way-you-want-it sex."

Duncan felt his mind take another spin. He was

skilled at getting into people's minds, but Piper's had to be the most fascinating one he'd ever encountered.

"If we can do it anytime we want, maybe we'll get it out of our systems. At the very least, I can think about RPK or the jerk who sent me those flowers instead of how I'm going to keep myself from jumping you."

When he said nothing, she frowned at him. "Well, what do you think?"

He registered the annoyance that laced her tone, but thinking had pretty much gone by the wayside. Not that it had done him much good so far. Thinking was what had kept him hesitating. Thinking had kept him away from her for seven long years. "Is there a difference between monkey sex and buddy sex?"

It took a full two beats for her to answer him. Then a grin lit up her features. "I can't say I'm an expert at either." She stripped out of her T-shirt as she walked toward him. "There's only one way to find out."

He couldn't take his eyes off the red lace bra. Until she pulled down her jeans and he saw the matching bikinis. And any brain cells still working clicked completely off when she climbed onto his lap and took his mouth with hers.

He had no choice but to wait out the first jolt. Then he greedily absorbed the second and third as she threaded her fingers through his hair and began to use her teeth on his lips—teasing, tormenting, torturing.

Nipping on his earlobe, she whispered, "I've been wanting to do this since I walked into the room."

Ditto. He wanted to say the words out loud, but her mouth was busy on his again.

"Oh, mmm," she murmured as if she'd just discovered a flavor she'd been craving.

He certainly had. *You,* he thought. *Only you.*

Sensations simply battered him and he relished each one. The softness of her thighs pressed against his waist. Her scent, feminine and filled with secrets. The low husky sounds that hummed in her throat and sizzled straight to his loins. The scrape of her nails as she flipped open the buttons of his golf shirt, then tugged it loose from his pants.

Together, they stripped off his shirt. Then her hands were on his flesh, inciting, arousing, demanding. Each trace of her fingers, each press of her palms brought a pleasure so intense, a weakness so delicious that he began to ache. She was aggressive in a way he'd never imagined or dreamed. She bewitched him in a way no other woman ever had.

When she drew back enough to slip her hands between them and tug open his belt, his fingers tangled with hers to free him. She found him, caressed him, and he lost his breath and probably part of his mind.

"Now," she said.

Her command triggered explosions inside of him. He thought he'd been prepared, but anticipation and reality were worlds apart. He covered both lace-covered breasts with his palms, heard the quick intake of her breath, felt the thunderous beat of her heart. And need clawed through him. She'd had a point about the white knight analogy, he thought. For the first time in his life, he'd wanted to just sweep a woman away on his charger to a place where he could keep her safe and make her his. More than that, he wanted to pull her to the floor and ravage her the way a warrior might claim the spoils of war.

But first, he wanted more. He needed more.

"My turn." He could barely hear the sound of his voice above the pounding of his blood, but he slid his

SAVE UP TO 25%

Subscribe to Blaze today and get 4 stories a month delivered to your door for 3, 6 or 12 months and gain up to 25% OFF! That's a fantastic saving of over £35!

MONTHS	FULL PRICE	YOUR PRICE	SAVING
3	£37.41	£31.77	15%
6	£74.82	£59.88	20%
12	£149.64	£112.20	25%

As a welcome gift we will also send you a FREE L'Occitane gift set worth £10

PLUS, by becoming a member you will also receive these additional benefits:

🌹 FREE Home Delivery

🌹 Receive new titles TWO MONTHS AHEAD of the shops

🌹 Exclusive Special Offers & Monthly Newsletter

🌹 Special Rewards Programme

No Obligation - You can cancel your subscription at any time by writing to us at Mills & Boon Book Club, PO Box 676, Richmond. TW9 1WU.

To subscribe, visit
millsandboon.co.uk/subscriptions

K2I

hands down to her waist and stood, bringing them both up and out of the chair. In one quick step, he braced her against the bookshelves and began to take what he needed.

EVEN THOUGH HIS HANDS MOVED like lightning, each quick, impatient caress sent a separate thrill rocketing through her. This was the part she'd never gotten to in the fantasies she'd penned. How could she have known?

More. Had she said it or merely thought it?

His hands moved between them to flip open her bra. Then he lowered his mouth and devoured. Each flick of his tongue, each scrape of his teeth brought a sharp, edgy shaft of pleasure.

Too much. Too much. Her heart had never beat so fast. Her body had never pulsed with so much life. But even as she reeled in a tidal wave of pleasures, all she craved was more. More.

Suddenly his mouth was gone. So were his hands.

She dug her nails into his shoulders and dragged in a breath. "Don't stop."

But he was already carrying her away from the bookcase and suddenly her feet were on the floor.

"I want to slow things down," he said.

"Why?" She gripped his shoulder and rose up on her toes. "Fast was great."

He framed her face with his hands. "Because I've waited seven years, and you did say something about any way I want it?"

When she nodded, he drew them both down so that they were kneeling and facing each other. "Let me show you." He combed his fingers slowly through her hair, drawing it back from her face. "I've been want-

ing to do this since the day of our parents' wedding.
You had your hair all twisted up in a fancy knot and I
wanted my hands in it. I wanted to taste you, too." Lowering his mouth slowly to hers, he did just that. But not
the way he had before. His lips barely brushed against
hers before he traced their shape with his tongue. And
just like that, he opened up a whole new world of sensations.

There was none of the flash and fire she'd felt before. Just softness and a glorious warmth that seemed
to be turning her blood thick. Each time the heat threat-
ened to flare, he would withdraw and change the angle
of the kiss as if he were searching for the perfect position and was determined to find it. Her mind began to
spin. Each time he changed the pressure of his mouth,
heat, glorious waves of it, shimmered right through to
the marrow of her bones. When her muscles went lax
and her hand dropped from his shoulder, he lowered
her slowly to the floor.

"Can't think," she whispered.

"Don't," he murmured against her mouth. "Just
feel."

Starting with her throat and shoulders, he took his
fingers and mouth on a journey down her body. Tasting, teasing, tempting. Sensations swamped her. Each
one carried her further and further beyond what she'd
ever imagined. Shouldn't she have known that the
brush of a fingertip over the tip of her breast would
make her tremble? Or that the scrape of a fingernail at
the back of her knee could make her moan? Or that the
feathering of his breath at her waist would make her
heart skip and race? No one had ever made her want
or need this way.

Fire and ice rippled over her nerve endings at the

same time that a flame flickered to life in her center and sent sparks spreading in a slow burn through her system. When he slipped a finger into her, she gasped his name as the unspeakable pleasure rushed through her. Then she fell weightlessly, bonelessly, and even as she did, he used his mouth on her and sent her soaring again. And again. There was nothing, no one but him. He could have asked anything of her. She would have refused him nothing. But all he did was give her more.

WHEN HE DREW BACK, HE WATCHED her in the thin shafts of sunlight as he hurriedly dealt with the rest of his clothes and slipped on protection. Her skin was sheened with moisture, her hair spread out on the floor, her eyes dazed and on his.

"Now," she whispered.

That one word shredded whatever thin grasp he still had on his control and triggered a series of explosions inside of him. The craving that had been building for so long had become so huge that he wasn't going to survive another second unless he filled her.

When he did, she cried out from the shock, from the intensity of the pleasure, and he felt his control snap. As he drove into her in fast, desperate thrusts, she matched him move for move. Heat became intense. Glorious. The pace was fast. Furious.

They were in a race, one that everything depended on, and they were neck and neck. The speed was insane, the pleasure outrageous. They both cried out as they reached the finish line together. He heard his name blend with hers before reality faded completely.

WHEN PIPER FINALLY OPENED HER eyes, she was lying on the floor of the library staring up at the ceiling two stories above. Her mind was gradually swimming back to reality, and she wasn't sure she could move. It wasn't just the fact that Duncan's arm and leg were pinning her down. She'd just never felt so relaxed, so spent. So…right?

No. Quickly, she pictured her bottle and corked up that little idea. Sex on demand was the perfect fantasy. No strings. No expectations. That was the deal she'd made with Duncan and herself.

At least she hoped they'd both agreed to it. She'd done most of the talking before she'd climbed onto his lap and conversation had pretty much ceased. She wasn't even clear on how much time had passed since she'd first entered the library. Minutes? Surely not hours. The slant of the sun through the windows hadn't shifted that much. And the dust motes had returned to their slow dance.

Still, she couldn't work up the will to move. She'd never noticed before that the ceiling was intricately carved and painted with some sort of scene; she couldn't imagine a more delightful way to have discovered its beauty. She felt her lips curve at the thought. So at least some part of her body was working.

Duncan stirred at her side. She angled her head, pleased to discover that it was also working, and met his eyes. For just a moment, she lost track of time again and there was just the two of them. Nothing else. No one else. She could have lain there just like that for a long time.

Too dangerous, she thought and searched for something to say.

Duncan beat her to it. "Do you think that qualified as monkey sex?"

She blinked, and then smiled at him. "I highly doubt that monkeys know how to do what you just did."

"Thanks, I think." He kissed the tip of her nose, then drew back to study her for a moment. He'd never felt so relaxed with her before. He wasn't sure he'd felt this comfortable with any woman. "You surprise me." Stunned would have been a more accurate word, he thought. And when he saw the slight frown flicker over her face, he gave her a quick hug. "In a good way." In every way. She'd been wild in a way he'd never imagined. And more responsive than he'd ever dreamed. "I don't think I'll ever look at this library—or any library—in quite the same way again."

The smile lit her face again. "Me, neither. So…are we in agreement?"

"About what?" For a moment he'd become totally focused on the way the light played over her features.

"About my proposal—sex on demand. It's the best solution to what's happening between us. It'll keep everything simple and neat."

Duncan traced a finger along her jaw line, felt her tremble. "You like simple." He liked it himself. Especially in his personal life, he'd always preferred it to complicated. But whatever they called it, he knew that what he'd just begun with Piper MacPherson was going to be as complicated as hell. He lifted the strap of her bra, rubbed the red lace between his finger and thumb. Who would have thought that beneath those conservative suits she was wearing something this… provocative?

"Duncan." She raised her hands to clasp the sides of his head, then waited for his eyes to meet hers. "I need you to focus on this because we have a lot on our plates.

We should get at least this part settled, and I have the feeling that half of your mind is on something else."

"It is," he said. "But I can multitask." There was some satisfaction in seeing her eyes widen as he fished into the pocket of his jeans to get another condom, then sheath himself in it. "If I recall, our deal is sex on demand, anytime, anyplace?"

"Yes."

"Okay then." He settled himself between her legs and then entered her in one smooth stroke. "This time it's going to be a long, slow ride."

And it was.

7

TAKING A HIKE HAD BEEN Duncan's idea. Piper had been motivated to agree when she realized that after making love three times, she would have been perfectly content to lie curled up with him on one of the couches in the library until they'd recovered enough for round four.

The sex on demand she'd fantasized about at nineteen was supposed to be convenient, not addicting. One of its benefits was they should actually be able to get some work done. So far they hadn't made much headway in the Lightman files. So it was probably a good idea to take a break and clear their heads.

It was one of those perfect days in the Adirondacks. The sun was high in the sky, the lake a perfectly matching blue below them. By the time she'd showered and changed, Duncan had already packed their lunch into a backpack and was waiting for her on the kitchen terrace. The man was meticulously organized.

His pace was brisk, but in spite of the fact that his legs were longer, she had no problem keeping up with him. The path he'd chosen was a familiar one that wound upward through the woods to the cliff face bordering the lake.

"Have you visited those old caves lately?" Duncan asked.

"No." She'd run along the cliffs frequently when she was in high school, but she'd never climbed down to revisit the caves after that summer he and his brothers had visited. She shot him a sideways glance. Maybe he'd forgotten how she'd frozen on the cliff face that day. "It was never one of my favorite places. If you'll recall, playing damsel in distress wasn't exactly my cup of tea."

"I do. After the first time we played pirates there, Reid and I tried to talk Cam out of playing it again. We thought it was too dangerous for you girls."

"Good thing you didn't tell us that. And I take it you didn't convince Cam, either."

He laughed as they came to the part of the cliff path that cut inland through the woods for a bit. "Not much chance of that. Cam was attracted to adventure and danger even back then. And Reid and I were certainly not immune to it. Plus, we got to take turns killing Cam in order to win back the treasure and rescue little Nell. Not a bad day's work. We did reach a compromise on the safety issue. After the first time, Reid made sure that Nell always drew the short straw and then offered to climb with her to the cave before you or Adair jumped in to protect her yourself."

Piper thought back, seeing the game through a different lens now. "As I recall, Reid spent a lot of his time that whole summer making sure that Nell was safe."

Duncan nodded. "Six was a little young to be rock climbing, not to mention some of the other things we did, and it turned out to be good practice for him. Even at ten, he already knew he wanted to go into the Secret Service. Now he's working on the vice president's detail."

She heard the pride in his voice and asked, "When did you know you wanted to be FBI?"

There were a couple of beats of silence before he glanced sideways at her and replied. "I probably decided the day the FBI came to our house and arrested my father for embezzling from his family's investment firm."

Surprise had her stumbling. But Duncan gripped her arm just in time to help her regain her balance. "How old were you?"

"Nine. It was the summer before we all came here. My father had always put his business as his first priority, especially after my brothers and I were born. He traveled and entertained a lot. He even kept an apartment in Manhattan. Every time he came home for any length of time, he would make my mother very unhappy."

He took a bottle of water out of the backpack, handed it to her, then fished another one out for himself. "I'd hear her crying in the middle of the night, and I felt helpless because there wasn't anything I could do."

She studied him as he sipped water. "Makes sense that you'd want to protect her. So you admired the FBI agents who took him away and wanted to grow up to be like them."

He began to walk again, this time veering off the path to take a shortcut to the cliffs. "I may not have been fully aware of it at the time, but I wanted to know what made someone do what my father did. Not just the stealing part. Greed is one of the things that makes the world go round. I wanted to know why he made my mom cry."

Understanding moved through her and tightened something around her heart. "So you were attracted to behavioral sciences."

"Ultimately." They stepped out of the trees into the sunshine. A few feet away, the earth fell away in a sheer drop to a strip of sandy beach below. "Sorry to put a dent in your white knight theory."

He hadn't. But she was prevented from pointing that out to him when her cell phone rang.

He put a hand on her arm before she could answer the call. "I meant to tell you before. Don't let anyone know where you are—not even your boss. I'll explain."

A glance at her caller ID told her that it was Abe. Guilt moved through her when she realized that she hadn't bothered to check her messages since they'd arrived at the castle. That wasn't like her at all. "Hello?"

"Piper, where are you?"

It wasn't Abe but an annoyed Richard Starkweather, her coworker. And he was using Abe's cell phone. "Hi, Richard. Is Abe all right?"

"Where are you? I stopped by your apartment to check on you last night and you didn't answer. So far, I've left three messages on your cell." There was concern in his voice, but beneath it, she heard a trace of annoyance.

"I've been…busy."

"Very busy," Duncan murmured in a voice only she could hear. She made the mistake of meeting Duncan's eyes and the glint of laughter had her choking back on a laugh.

"Where are you?" Richard asked again.

"Where's Abe and why are you using his cell phone?" she countered.

"Abe asked me to call. We need your help on the Bronwell case. You have to make yourself available. We need to know where you are."

Piper kept her tone patient. "Richard, you were in the meeting I had with Abe yesterday afternoon. I'm taking a few days off at Abe's request. As far as the Bronwell case goes, I turned over all my files to you. It's all there. Why aren't you using your own phone?"

"Because you haven't returned any of my calls. Obviously, you were avoiding me. If I have questions, I need to get a hold of you."

She bit down hard on annoyance. "You've got hold of me now. What do you want?"

"How long will you be out of town?"

"Until the publicity fades and Abe thinks I can return." But in her head she said, *Until I can take over second chair again. Then you won't have to ask me any questions.*

"Sorry, I'm losing the connection," she said aloud. Then she broke the connection and took a long drink of her water.

"You don't like Richard," Duncan said.

She paced away, and then whirled to come back to him. "Actually, I think it's the other way around. In Richard Starkweather's view, I have two strikes against me. He was Abe's right-hand man until I was hired, and then I refused to go out with him. Several times."

"What was the I'm-so-concerned-about-you act he put on in your apartment yesterday?"

"That was about impressing Abe."

"Some men don't take either rejection or competition well. Does he dislike you enough to stage that scene yesterday morning and send the flowers?"

Piper stared at him. "Good heavens, no. Why would he?"

"To get you out of the way so that he could take over second chair at the Bronwell trial. My boss, Adrienne, suspects that someone in Abe's office may have leaked the fact that you wrote the brief—to either the Macks family or to one of the other victim's families. No one in my office was aware of your involvement. I didn't even know you worked for Abe."

"I can't believe that Richard would do something like that," she said.

"Abe's a suspect, too. It's very convenient that the media is focused on you now and not him. He can go forward with the Bronwell trial with a cleaner slate, so to speak."

"That's ridiculous. Abe would never do anything like that."

"Maybe not. But until we figure out who staged that scene in your apartment and is sending you flowers, my boss would like to keep your location a secret, even from your coworkers."

"How? This is my home. Even Richard could guess that I might come here."

"Yeah." Duncan smiled slowly. "I've given that some thought. I didn't mention it to Adrienne, but it might work to our advantage if our RPK imitator does follow us up here. In D.C., it's fairly easy to remain anonymous. Up here, strangers are remarked upon. Earlier today, I spoke with Sheriff Skinner in Glen Loch and filled him in on the situation. He's putting the word out through Edie at her diner. He claims she's his best investigator."

Piper didn't like the fact that their conversation had started the nerves dancing in her stomach again. "I want this all to be over." She shifted her gaze down to the lake and let the view diffuse some of her anger. "But I'm not going to run any farther than this."

Duncan got that. He'd seen that quality in her when she'd been eight and he'd come upon her clinging to the cliff face for dear life. His heart had nearly stopped. But she'd held on until he'd been able to reach her, and she hadn't panicked. Then she'd followed his directions like a trooper as they'd climbed down together.

He placed his hands on her shoulders and turned her to face him. "You'll be fine here. Thanks to whoever it was paying nocturnal visits to the castle library, the security is currently CIA approved, and Vi says that Daryl Garnett will be here for the weekend because of that photo shoot. As head of the CIA's domestic operations, he's the best when it comes to white knights. But so are you."

She frowned at him. "What are you talking about?"

"That time you had to play damsel in distress in the cave all afternoon? You did that to protect Nell. And you told a bald-faced lie when you claimed that you'd always dreamed of being rescued."

"Maybe."

"Whoever this guy is who's sending you flowers, he picked the wrong person to mess with. But I suggested we come out here to get your mind off everything else for a while. And I have an idea of just how we can do that."

She stared at him. "You want to have sex here?"

With a grin he glanced around. They were on the steepest part of the cliff and while there was no one in plain sight, anyone with a good pair of binoculars or a camera with a telephoto lens could see them. "Tempting, but that's not what I had in mind."

Instead, he swung the backpack off his shoulder and sat down. "I thought we might share some lunch before we climb down to explore those caves."

"You want to climb down to the caves." She walked over to him and took one of the sandwiches he held out. "Why?"

He sat down on the grass near the cliff edge and gestured for her to join him as he pulled out his own sandwich. "I want to check something out." He explained his theory about it being Eleanor who'd hidden her dowry.

She took the time to chew and swallow the first bite of her sandwich while she mulled it over. "You're profiling her."

"I suppose I am in a way. I'm looking at what we know and trying to theorize what might have happened."

"Okay, I see your point. Eleanor wore the sapphire in her wedding portrait, and there's no record, either visual or written, of their existence after she died. So it's logical to think she'd be the one who hid them. It also stands to reason that if she split the earrings and hid just one of them in the stone arch, she hid the two other pieces of her dowry elsewhere. Otherwise, why split them up in the first place?"

"Exactly. And if she hid one of them outside the castle, it seems logical that she'd hide the other pieces somewhere else, also."

"Very logical," Piper said around a second bite of sandwich. "That's why we're here. You figure Angus would have known about the caves. This was land he chose. It stands to reason he would have explored all of it. Heck, it didn't take you and your brothers more than a week to find them. So Eleanor would have known about the caves also. You showed them to Adair and Nell and me the same day you discovered them."

"Right."

"But if any part of the Stuart Sapphires is in the caves, surely one of you would have found it."

"We scoured both of those caves, but we were looking for some kind of treasure box, not something as small as a leather pouch."

"Both of them?" She turned to meet his eyes. "Didn't any of you ever look in the third cave?"

Duncan stared at her. "There's a third cave down there? We only knew about two. How did you find a third one?"

"Boredom is a strong motivator. The tunnel leading to it was pretty much blocked off by a boulder in the second cave. I couldn't budge it, but I managed to squeeze behind it. The third cave is the biggest one and it was empty. But then I wasn't focused on finding Eleanor's dowry at the time. Finish your sandwich and let's climb down and take a look around."

PIPER'S ARMS WERE ACHING AS she wedged her fingers in between two rocks and searched for the next foothold. She could do this. She wasn't a scared eight-year-old anymore.

"To your left," Duncan called from below her.

In true white knight style, he'd pointed out the narrow rock ledge about one hundred feet below them, and then he'd insisted on going first and she'd let him. She was betting he'd already reached it. He'd been halfway there when she'd swung her legs over the edge. But she didn't dare look down to check his progress.

"A little more to the left," Duncan called.

Her shoe found the opening, then slid out. The sudden shift in her weight had her fingers gripping the rocks and her heart leaping up to lodge in her throat.

"You've almost got it," Duncan called.

What was the matter with her? This wasn't any different from climbing to the ground from her balcony. Except there weren't any vines and it wasn't soft ground that she would land on if she slipped.

"Don't worry. The ledge is directly below you now. If you slip, you won't fall far."

Good to know. If he was telling the truth. She glanced up at how far she'd come and realized that it would take as much effort to go back up as continue.

And wasn't that exactly what Macbeth had realized during his famous dagger speech?

"Shakespeare always comes back to haunt you," she muttered.

"What?" Duncan called up.

"Nothing." This had actually been easier when she was eight. And with that depressing realization came a surge of determination.

Muscles straining, she jabbed her toe into the crevice and lowered herself another foot.

"Directly below you, there's a flat rock you can step on," Duncan called.

The instant her foot connected with the narrow ledge, she heard a rumble above her. Pebbles and small rocks clattered down. The first one hit her knuckles so sharply that she nearly lost her grip. Another bounced off her shoulder, and as she glanced up, a third grazed the side of her head. She had to blink dust out of her eyes, but for a moment, she thought she saw a figure on the cliff above. By the time she blinked again, Duncan was at her side, his arm around her waist, his voice murmuring. "On three, we're going to jump. The ledge is just below us. Ready?"

She managed a nod as more dust and stones rained on them.

"One…two…three."

The drop was short, the landing hard. Then he pushed her into the low-ceilinged cave, using his body to block the debris still rattling down.

"You all right?" he asked as the noise subsided. His arms were wrapped tightly around her and her back was against stones. For a moment, she simply held on. She'd move as soon as her heart stopped pounding. Just one more minute.

She made herself breathe. In. Out. "I'm fine." Other than feeling like Chicken Little, she was. Still, she clung for one more moment, trying not to think of what might have happened if he hadn't climbed up to get her. "I have to admit that white knights come in handy."

But it would be very dangerous to depend on one too much. She met his eyes. "I'm pretty sure I saw someone on the top of the cliff."

"Me, too." Then he put a hand over her mouth and for a moment they both listened hard. The shower of rocks and pebbles had stopped. All she could hear in the silence was the call of a gull.

Duncan whispered, "Stay here."

Then he rose and moved to the mouth of the cave. The moment he stepped out onto the ledge, she rose to her feet, but he stepped back in before she could reach him.

"There's no one up there now, but if we go out on that ledge or try to climb up, we could be sitting ducks. I figured we'd have more time before someone tracked us here." He pulled out his cell, and then swore under his breath. "No signal."

"Well, as I see it, we have two alternatives. We can take our chances surviving more rock slides and climb down to the beach. Not my favorite plan. Or we can go ahead with our original idea," she said. "We did come here to search the cave and look for Eleanor's dowry. And since we risked life and limb to get this far, I say we forge ahead."

Duncan gave it some thought. The woman had guts and she was giving voice to his own instincts were telling him. "Whoever we saw up on the top of the cliff may decide to follow us."

"And run the risk of revealing himself or even getting caught?"

"Point taken." He pulled a flashlight out of his backpack and handed it to her. "You lead the way."

"This may be a tight squeeze for you. We're both bigger than we used to be."

"I'll manage."

Piper switched on the light and swept it over the walls. The area they stood in was roughly five feet deep, perhaps seven wide. The tunnel they entered offered even less space, and while she could walk upright, Duncan had to hunch over.

"Just a warning," she said. "If I see anything that moves, I'm screaming."

Duncan chuckled. "But you won't be running away."

"Correct." She stopped dead in her tracks when the tunnel widened into the second cave. "This is different."

Over her shoulder, Duncan saw the large boulder and the rocks of various sizes that now partially filled the space. Beyond the pile up of debris was an opening that appeared to be another tunnel.

"Look." She stepped to the side and ran her flashlight over everything so that Duncan could see. "That big boulder was blocking the tunnel to the third cave the last time I was in here."

"It's been almost two decades," Duncan said. "Plenty of time for things to shift around. You still game to lead the way?"

"Absolutely." She placed a hand against the wall to brace herself as she negotiated the fallen rocks toward the other tunnel.

Duncan had to hunch down when the ceiling abruptly lowered, and before long, the tunnel began to slope upward. In his mind, he tried to picture where they were headed in terms of the land above them. Just when he'd decided they were walking roughly in the direction of the castle, the tunnel took a sharp turn to the left, then widened abruptly into a larger room that allowed him to fully stand for the first time.

"Here's the third cave," she announced as she moved the flashlight slowly around the space.

He spotted the small pile of rocks at the same instant that she froze the beam of light on it. The pile lay near a good-size boulder that had shifted and evidently tumbled loose from the arch of yet another tunnel directly across from the one they'd stepped out of.

"I never saw that tunnel before," she said. "It must have been completely blocked."

"Alba found the leather pouch containing the earring in a pile of rocks that had tumbled loose when lightning struck the stone arch," Duncan said, urging her forward. They both dropped to their knees and began sorting through the pile near the side of the boulder.

Then they began to work on the stones that were loose at the sides of the newly opened tunnel. Each one they dislodged seemed to loosen more.

"Got something," Piper said. The sound of her voice echoed in the space. When she pulled it out, Duncan recognized the leather pouch immediately.

"It matches the one that your aunt Vi and Adair found the first earring in," he murmured.

Piper set it between them on the stone floor and then met his eyes. "Your theory. Maybe you should do the honors."

"No. You're the one who found it." Another part of Eleanor's dowry would be inside, he was certain. But he still held his breath as she folded back the flap of leather and reached in. Even in the dim light, the gold of the earring glistened and the sapphire glowed. She lifted it out and offered it to him. When he clasped his hands around hers, the stone flashed even brighter, and Duncan felt that same, strong, sure connection to Piper that he'd first experienced on his mother's wedding day. Time seemed to stand still.

Then they heard a clatter of rocks.

"Shhh," Duncan breathed in answer to the question in Piper's eyes. Only time would tell if the noise had been caused by some of the rocks they'd loosened on their journey or by someone who'd followed them.

Seconds passed—five, ten, fifteen. Just as he was about to breathe again, there was a second scrape and clatter of stones. He leaned closer to whisper, "Someone's in the tunnel we just came through."

If he'd been alone, he would have doused the light and waited at the side of the opening they'd just stepped through. But he wasn't alone, and he wanted a better tactical advantage and more data before he initiated a confrontation.

He took the earring out of her hand and secured it in the leather pouch. Then he slipped it beneath his T-shirt and tucked it into his back pocket. Finally, he picked up the flashlight and rose to check out the tunnel the stones and boulder had tumbled from. It was smaller than either of the ones they'd walked through. But for now, it would offer some cover.

"We'll have to be quiet. C'mon." He spoke the words lower than a whisper, but she rose and gripped his outstretched hand. Ducking his head, he led the way into the cramped space. Being quiet was easier said than done. But he let out the breath he'd been holding when he noted the rocks that had tumbled loose near the entrance gave way to smoother stones in a matter of a few yards. The bad news was that he couldn't see a curve in the tunnel yet, and he had no idea where it would take them.

But he could swear he felt the warmth of the sapphire through the thickness of the leather that enclosed it. Pausing, he glanced back. They'd come far enough that he could no longer see the room they'd left. But there was another clatter of rocks. He moved on, and within a few steps, the beam of the light illuminated the curve he was hoping for.

Drawing her around it, he spoke in a hurried whisper. "I'm going to have to turn off the flashlight, but first, get the gun out of my backpack."

She didn't hesitate a beat, but handled the task with the same ease and efficiency that she might have exerted if he'd asked for his water bottle. When he held out his hand, she placed the gun in it. "Now, switch places with me."

Once she had, he turned off the light, pitching them into total darkness. And waited. While they did, Duncan put himself into the mind of the person or persons who'd followed them into the cave. Whoever it was had to know that Piper wasn't alone. If it was the person who was sending the flowers and the death threats, why would he or she make this move? Setting that minor avalanche of stones off the cliff—*that* he could see. But following them in here seemed reckless. Desperate.

For now, he and Piper had a slight advantage. They weren't moving. And there was a very good chance that their pursuer still was.

At first the silence was so total that Duncan was sure he could hear the beat of his own heart. Then he heard what he'd been waiting for—the sound of more rocks being dislodged.

But which ones?

In his mind, he pictured the route they'd taken— the first pile of stones had been in the second of the caves he and his brother had played in as kids. So that's where their pursuer must have been earlier. That meant he had to be in the cave they'd just left, the one that Piper had discovered, where they'd found the earring.

Close, Duncan thought. He listened hard.

Nothing. No more rocks shifted. And there was no conversation, not even a whisper sounded. Then the darkness in front of him lightened fractionally. Whoever it was had seen the tunnel and was shining a light into it. Beside him, Piper placed a hand on his back to indicate she'd seen it, too, but she remained perfectly still. Perfectly silent.

A lone pursuer, Duncan guessed, who was weighing options. And listening for a sound—just as he and Piper were. To go forward or retreat? Pursuing them any farther was risky. Especially if your quarry knew you were coming. And in the silence, he had to at least suspect they did.

Rocks tumbled again. Behind him, he heard Piper suck in a quiet breath. But the darkness was total once more. The next sound of stones came from farther away. Still, Duncan didn't move and neither did she.

He'd counted to twenty when Piper breathed. "He left."

"That's the good news."

"What's the bad?"

"We can't go out the way we came in. Whoever it is could be waiting. And that's not the worst scenario."

"It can get worse?"

"He could suspect we're listening, and he could have retreated just to throw us off. Even now, he could be doubling back. That's what I'd do." He took her arm and urged her in front of him. "I'll bring up the rear just in case."

8

<hr>

WITH ONE HAND PRESSED against the wall of the tunnel and the other out in front of her, Piper concentrated on putting one foot in front of the other, testing each step as she went. *Just think about that*, she told herself. *Worry later about who might have followed them into the cave and why.*

The stones beneath her palm were cool to the touch, some smoother than others. She couldn't see a thing. And this tunnel could dead-end in front of them in a Hollywood minute.

Don't think about that. Instead, she pictured what the two of them must look like. With one hand clamped to her shoulder, Duncan was totally relying on her to lead the way. The perfect image of the blind leading the blind. Much better to think about that than to worry about the fact that his other hand was probably gripping that very large gun she'd found in his backpack.

Seconds ticked into minutes, and she felt as if they were moving at a snail's pace. But Duncan said nothing, and he didn't have a problem with telling her what to do. She heard a whack, then Duncan's quick intake of breath.

"Hit my head," he breathed. "Need a minute."

She used the time to reach up. The rocks overhead were only inches away, which meant that Duncan had to be practically crab-walking. In the short silence that stretched between them, she heard only the sound of their breathing.

Then came the faint sound of rocks hitting other rocks.

"He's in the cave we just left," Duncan whispered. "When I see a light behind us, I'll let you know."

Oh, good, Piper thought. One more thing to be nervous about. What would they do then? Run?

No, she wasn't going to go there. In her mind, she corked up all the worries and started forward again. She was just going to pretend she was on her morning run—which she hadn't had a chance to get in yet.

In the next seemingly endless stretch of minutes, she imagined that she was passing the shoe store, the bookshop. All routine except she found that the floor of the tunnel was climbing upward more steeply. The walls had begun to press in, and they were suddenly not just cool to the touch, but damp.

"The walls," she whispered. "Touch them."

His hand left her shoulder for a moment. "Wet. But we're not headed toward the lake."

"No." This time she was the one who whacked her head hard. Stars spun in front of her eyes as she sank to her knees.

"You all right?"

"I think so."

Duncan's arm was around her, and she felt his chest pressed hard against her back. Panic bubbled up. Whatever she'd rammed into had come up fast. Had they finally reached a dead end? She blinked once and then twice. It wasn't just stars she was seeing. Ahead of her light penetrated the absolute darkness. And when she glanced down, she thought she could just make out her hands on the floor of the tunnel.

In the silence, they could hear the scrape of something against stone. A shoe? A shoulder?

But escape was in front of them. Piper was sure of it. "There's got to be an opening up ahead," she breathed. "It'll be faster if we crawl."

Crawl they did. The incline was sharper now, but they were making better time. Rocks scraped against her hands. And she had to slow her pace twice to get the sweat out of her eyes. But the light ahead grew steadily stronger and suddenly she could hear the sound of water above the pounding of her heart.

The area around them suddenly widened, and the shaft of light pouring in from above was blinding. She was still blinking against it when she heard Duncan grunting behind her. Turning, she saw he had his shoulder against a rock the size of a small boulder. In seconds he had it blocking the space they'd just crawled through. "Just in case," he gasped.

Then he gripped her waist and thrust her toward the opening above them. It wasn't large, but the fresh air nearly made her giddy. She spotted the root of a pine. She clamped one hand over it and dug the fingers of her other into the soil. Breathing hard, she pulled, twisted and muscled her way onto her belly. For one long moment, she was tempted to just lie there on the ground.

But Duncan still had to get out. His push on her foot gave her the extra boost she needed to crawl all the way out. Rolling, she shoved to her feet in time to see the backpack appear in the opening. Then Duncan wiggled out. *Good grief,* she thought. Was he some kind of superhero? He gave her no chance to catch her breath. Instead, he said, "Help me with this one."

Together, they rolled the largest of the nearby rocks to cover the hole they'd crawled out of. "I don't think they'll get past the other blockade, but just in case."

Piper bent over, braced her hands on her knees and concentrated on taking deep breaths. She was on her second one when Duncan grabbed her hand. "Where are we?"

She had to take a second to get her bearings. They'd climbed out of a wall of rocks that rose high to form a ledge. That, plus a glimpse of the pond beyond and the thundering noise of water falling, told her exactly where they were. "Tinker's Falls."

Duncan gaze swept the small clearing. "The pond. That's where we used to play water polo."

"It's where you and your brothers used to play 'Drown the MacPhersons,'" she said drily. "And imitate various superheroes by diving off the rock ledge."

"We were ten."

"You were jerks," she said.

As he reacquainted himself with the space, he'd already begun to get into the mind of the person who'd followed them. "How far away are the cliffs and the lake?"

She was still dragging in air, fighting for oxygen as much as he was, but she knew exactly what he was thinking. Jerking her head toward the thick wall of tall pines to their left, she said, "Three minutes, tops. You think we can cut through the woods and beat him back there? Catch him?"

"That's the plan. Are you game?"

Her answer was to tighten her grip on his hand and lead the way into the woods. The trees stretched high into the sky, blocking out any breeze and perfuming the air with their scent. In spite of the fact that there was no clearly delineated path, she set the pace at a jog, zigging and zagging between and around thick tree trunks. Twigs snapped underfoot, and brambles snatched at their clothes. Together they leaped over a fallen log that blocked their path.

THREE MINUTES, SHE'D SAID. As they continued to tick by, Duncan pictured the chain of tunnels and the caves beneath them. If their pursuer had turned back at the first boulder he'd shoved into place, he could be almost back to the ledge by now. But there was always the chance that he'd wasted time trying to shove it aside. Duncan could only hope for the latter. That kind of desperation, obsession, would be consistent with the profile he'd already tentatively posed in his mind.

The pines were suddenly thicker, the brush denser. Piper slowed their pace, but she didn't change direction. "Not far now," she promised.

Seconds later, they stepped into full sunlight again, only a hundred yards or so from the place where'd they'd eaten their sandwiches earlier. Keeping her hand gripped tight in his, he raced with her to the spot just in time to see a figure climbing down the rocks toward the thin ribbon of sand that bordered the lake. He gauged the distance, weighing the possibility of pursuit.

"Go," Piper said, her breath coming in huge gasps.

"No." He couldn't leave her alone. Not until she was safe again. He'd already been too careless today. "There'll be another time." He was going to make sure of it.

The figure below reached the sand. He was wearing a hooded sweatshirt that prevented them from getting a good look at his features. Without glancing up, he raced off along the lakeshore in the direction away from the castle. Seconds later he disappeared around a sharp curve in the beach.

Suddenly, all the fear that he'd pushed aside when they'd been in the tunnels and while they'd raced through the woods hit him again. With one rough move, he pulled Piper around to face him.

Her face was streaked with sweat and dirt, her hair tangled. And it struck him so hard that for a moment everything else faded. He could have lost her. He streaked his hands from her shoulders to frame her face. The instant he lowered his mouth to hers, he fell away from the fear and into her. And he wanted to fall further. With her mouth hot and avid on his, he wanted to keep on descending into a world where there was only the two of them.

Some lingering awareness of their surroundings had him gripping her hips and carrying her into the cover of the woods. At the first tree that blocked his path, he stopped, pressed her against it and felt his mind shatter like fine crystal. For several seconds, he forgot everything but the strength of that tight, lithe body molded to his, the movement of her mouth. And he couldn't seem to get enough of any of it.

He drew back and felt his lungs burn as he dragged in air. Some of the oxygen made its way to his brain. There was an important reason he should get her back to the castle. But he couldn't quite latch onto it. Not when she plunged her fingers into his hair and sank her teeth into his shoulder.

"I want you," he managed. "I need to touch you."

"Magic words," she murmured and dragged his mouth back to hers. Their thoughts were completely in tune. And for one moment, his hands seemed to be everywhere, tough, impatient, relentless. The speed, the roughness, delighted even as it spurred her on.

Something ripped. Her clothes or his—she couldn't be sure, but her hands found flesh at last. His skin was burning, damp and so smooth. His body was so tight, his muscles bunching under her hands. Hunger spiked. Greed dominated. She simply couldn't get enough. Using teeth and hands, she feasted.

Her breath caught as he dragged her to the ground. Then they rolled, legs tangling, mouths and fingers searching, groping, bruising while they fought with their remaining clothes. As desperate as he was to taste and to possess, she rolled with him again. Their minds and desires were fused, locked on the same goal. Each second of delay, each obstacle they overcame—jeans, shoes, even those precious moments when he had to find the condom and sheath himself, brought its own separate, torturous thrill.

Duncan felt his muscles quiver as they rolled again. There had never been anyone he'd craved this way. Every inch, every curve, every tremble, every throaty whisper of his name only fueled the fire that had been building since he'd touched her last. Need sliced him, its razor-sharp edges cutting into his throat, his loins, his heart. He raised his head, meeting her eyes as he drove into her.

He felt her clamp around him and shuddered when she came. But he fought a vicious battle against his own release, dragging her up with him so that he was kneeling, her legs still wrapped around him. Then he gripped her hips, his fingers digging into her.

"Stay with me, Piper."

He wasn't sure he'd even said the words out loud. But those amber eyes opened, and he could see himself in their depths. She thought only of him. He thought only of her as he coaxed her into a rhythm, biting back the need to race until he knew she was with him. Only when he felt her clamp around him again, only when he heard her cry his name on her own release did he let himself fall with her.

DUNCAN COULDN'T BE SURE how long they lay sprawled there on the ground. She was in his arms, stretched along his length, and the feel of her, the fit of her body pressed to his was…right. Just as he'd always known it would be. What was new, what was spreading not like a fire but like a warm river through his blood, was the thought that he could have been happy to hold her just like this for a very long time.

And he couldn't afford to do that right now. Two sensations drove home that realization. One was the leather pouch pressing into his backside. The other, more annoying, was the insistent vibration of his cell phone against his left thigh.

In one smooth move, he shifted, lifting her onto his lap as he leaned back against a tree. She fit her head into the crook of his shoulder in a gesture he found so endearing that for another moment, he simply held on to her, ignoring his phone.

"This isn't working," she said.

Alarmed, he pressed a finger under her chin, tilting her head so that he could look into her eyes. "I know I was rough. Did I hurt you?"

"No. Even if you had, I'd let you do it again in a

second." She drew in a breath, let it out. "Just as soon as I catch my breath."

"What exactly isn't working?"

His cell phone vibrated again. He ignored it.

"That's what's not working," Piper said. "You're ignoring your cell phone. And I can't even think straight yet."

"Have to say, we're in the same boat there."

"The whole idea of the on-demand-sex fantasy is that it compartmentalizes sex so that it's less distracting. That's why I fantasized about it all those years ago. I wanted simple. We should be able to keep our eyes on the goal and do the work we came here to do. But you're currently ignoring your cell phone. And I haven't even checked mine yet. Plus, we just narrowly escaped from someone who may have wished us bodily harm."

She sighed and leaned her head against his shoulder again. "It should have been the perfect solution for us, but I can't seem to be near you without wanting to rip your clothes off."

Duncan laughed. He couldn't stop himself. She'd hit the nail on the head. And when she gave up and joined him, he squeezed her in a friendly hug. "Look on the bright side. Since we're both pretty much naked, that problem seems to be solved temporarily."

She gave his shoulder a punch. "Not funny." But the shared laughter was still clear in her voice. "We have to get serious and figure out who followed us into the cave and why."

"Those *are* the questions of the day," Duncan said. And they were enough to sober both of them.

"I think we can cross your favorite suspects, Abe and Richard, off the list," Piper said.

"Agreed." He couldn't picture either one of them scaling down those rocks so effortlessly. And how would either of them have found the time to come to the castle? "They could have hired someone, mind you."

"Why? If your theory is right, they've achieved their goal. I'm out of town. Richard's sitting second chair. Why follow us? But…"

"But what?"

"What if we're looking at this from the wrong angle?" She raised her head enough to meet his eyes. "They're not the only ones who might have wanted me out of D.C. Maybe the whole point of that staged scene and the flower deliveries was to get me back up here to the castle?"

"I'm listening," Duncan murmured.

She rose from his lap and began to pace. "What if this is all about Eleanor's dowry?"

Duncan narrowed his eyes, following her train of thought. "The sapphires could very well be playing some role in this. Cam's theory is that whoever was visiting the library had some kind of inside information, something that makes him or her believe that the library holds the key to the location of Eleanor's dowry. But then lightning struck the stone arch and Adair found the first earring before he could unlock the secret."

"Had to be a bummer for him," Piper said.

"It gets worse. Cam set up extra security so he couldn't visit the library anymore. It's not a stretch to think that the library guy starts thinking there might be some link between you and your sisters and the rest of Eleanor's sapphires."

"Or he could see us as competition. Adair found the

first earring. Could be he's afraid Nell or I will beat him to the rest."

He had to admire the way her mind worked. Shifting the lens and looking at it from that angle made a great deal of sense. "Very possible. But then my guess is that the library guy wouldn't want you up here. So I'm still not convinced he was behind the scene in your apartment. But it's certainly in his interest to keep tabs on you now that you're here. And if he followed us from the castle earlier, he heard everything I told you about my theory of where that earring might have been hidden. But I don't think he could know for sure that we found it."

"So the guy in the hooded sweatshirt could be the library guy."

"I like it as a theory. Whoever he is, he's obsessed with finding Eleanor's sapphires. But we can't discount other possibilities. The guy who's sending you death threats could have easily caused that little avalanche. My suspicion is that he's someone who's really angry that you let Lightman out of jail. And he wants you to suffer at least part of what the victims suffered before they died. The fact that you left your apartment may have made him even angrier. Why not kick a few stones down on you? Or someone else could have followed us out to the cliffs, someone we haven't thought of yet. The key to being a good profiler is that you can't jump to premature conclusions."

"Great. You've already pointed out there's a target on my back. Now I can worry about the number of people taking aim at it."

Standing there naked in the slants of sunlight, she looked like Diana the Huntress. Was that why it hit him so hard again? All he knew was that she was beautiful in a way that made his heart take a long tumble. That was dangerous. Almost as dangerous as the image he'd planted in both their minds. And he had to keep focused on the fact that she was in danger.

Rising, he went to her and took her hands. "I want you to picture it. I want both of us to imagine the worst and hope for the best. We can't be certain yet that there isn't more than one thing going on here. In fact, I have a definite feeling that there is."

When his cell began to vibrate again, he released her so that he could retrieve his jeans and dig it out of his pocket. He checked the ID. "Adrienne."

"You're not answering your phone," she said.

"I am now. Good or bad news?"

Adrienne's sigh spoke volumes.

Duncan tipped the phone so that Piper could hear the bad news. "I'm letting Piper listen to what you have to say."

"The men I've assigned to keep tabs on Lightman have lost him. He hadn't made an appearance outside his place all morning. When my men checked his apartment about an hour ago, there was no sign of him. Last visual they had on him was yesterday around dinnertime."

Duncan's mind was racing. Maybe he'd been too quick to dismiss Lightman as the person who'd staged the scene in Piper's apartment.

But it was Piper who spoke the suspicion out loud. "Lightman is smart. He could have bought the wrong kind of sheet and used fresh rose petals just to throw us off."

Or to simply play with her mind, Duncan thought. He squeezed her hand as Adrienne continued, "If Lightman is targeting you, Ms. MacPherson, he'll have done his research. He'll know that your home is at Castle MacPherson."

"Keep me posted," Duncan said, and disconnected. Then he raised the hand he was holding to his lips. "I know. You're not going to run."

She met his eyes. "You're not going to try to change my mind?"

"Waste of time. I'm a Scot. We're thrifty. And I'm not sure it's the best option."

"I just wish our prime suspects were still Abe and Richard."

He grinned at her. "Me, too."

She released his hand and began to gather up their clothes, tossing his to him as she sorted through them. He was watching her pull her jeans on when she met his eyes and the Diana the Huntress look was there again.

He felt his heart tumble again.

"If Lightman comes after me, he's in for a surprise."

She was right about that. She was a very surprising woman. But he didn't intend to let Patrick Lightman anywhere near her.

9

THE ROAD TO HELL WAS PAVED with good intentions. Less than two hours later, Duncan pictured his most recent one being crushed by the wheels of his car as he parked it in front of Edie's Diner. The restaurant sat on the main street of Glen Loch, and its wide front window offered customers a view of the lake and Castle MacPherson across the water. From what he could see, the place hadn't changed. His mother had brought them to Edie's frequently during the summer that she'd worked on her book at the castle.

The setup inside was typically fifties and provided seating at tables, in red leather booths and on stools along a polished white counter. Beyond that, the kitchen was open to view. People, locals as well as tourists, could come to Edie's for the food and the latest in news and gossip. As he recalled, both were the best in town.

He and Piper had come for neither. They'd come to talk to Patrick Lightman.

Sheriff Skinner's call had come a half hour after they'd gotten back to the castle. By that time Piper had checked in with her aunt Vi and passed on the news about the earring, and Duncan had used the number Cam had given him to fill Daryl Garnett in on the discovery, as well as the person who'd followed them into the cave. Cam's boss didn't like it any more than he did. Daryl assured him that as soon as Vi finished her wedding presentation at the mall in Albany, they'd drive straight back to the castle.

He and Piper had been about to resume their work on the Lightman files when the castle phone had rung. Skinner's message had been brief. A man had just walked into his office and asked him to arrange a meeting with Piper.

The man had identified himself as Patrick Lightman.

Skinner had insisted that they meet at Edie's Diner. After turning off his car's engine, Duncan reached over the gearshift and linked his fingers with Piper's. "You don't have to go in." Earlier, he'd argued vehemently and unproductively that he could take the meeting for her. He'd already contacted Adrienne and informed her of Lightman's whereabouts.

"I'm going in. This is my chance to see him in person. He could say something, do something that will put me on the right track to sending him back to jail. Plus, I want to know why he's come all this way to see me. And why he's doing it in this public way."

That was one of the questions he'd given some thought to on the drive into town. "Cam has a great deal of respect for Skinner. Meeting here at Edie's will broadcast Lightman's presence to the entire local community. Within an hour of the time Lightman leaves the diner, everyone in town will know who he is and why he's here. If he's planning on staying in Glen Loch, everyone will have his description and be on the look-out for him."

"But it was Lightman's idea to approach Skinner rather than just knock on the castle door," Piper pointed out. "He doesn't have to report in to the sheriff. He's a free man."

"He's also a brilliant man. This way, if he hangs around no one can accuse him of stalking you. Even if that's his intention. We could be playing right into his hands."

Piper shook her head. "No. It doesn't fit his pattern to be so public. He's not here to stalk me. And he's not as smart as he thinks he is. He may be playing into our hands." She smiled at him. "He's a meticulous planner, but I'll bet he didn't expect me to bring an FBI profiler with me to this meeting."

His lips curved slightly. "You're trying to make me feel better about this."

"I'm trying to make me feel better, too." On impulse, she framed his face with her hands and pulled his mouth down for a quick kiss. But any temptation she felt to prolong the kiss and feel even better was halted by the sound of a voice hailing them from across the street.

"Ms. MacPherson?"

The man striding toward them was the handsome blond man who'd visited the castle that morning. Piper used the few seconds that it took her to climb out of Duncan's car to gather her thoughts and search for a name. "Mr. Arbogast. From *Architectural Digest*."

"Russell, please." His smile beamed. "I'm so happy to run into you like this. I was trying to get hold of you a couple of hours ago, but no one picked up the phone at the castle."

"Duncan and I were out for a while."

Russell nodded at Duncan. "Good to see you again, Mr. Sutherland. You're Piper's stepbrother, right?"

When she felt Duncan stiffen, she said, "Why did you call?"

"I hoped to schedule that interview you promised. That way you could give me your take on growing up in the castle that Angus MacPherson built for his true love. I'm particularly interested in the stone arch and its legend. We've made arrangements to do a feature on the old Campbell castle in Scotland, and we were thrilled to discover what must be the original stone arch in the garden."

"Really?" Piper asked.

"We're as certain as we can ever be about something like that. I could tell you all about it if you'd join me for dinner. I hear there's a lovely little restaurant over by the college with a porch that overlooks the lake."

"Ms. MacPherson has other plans for dinner," Duncan said. "And we're on our way to a meeting right now."

The next thing she knew Duncan was pulling her across the street. "Tomorrow," Piper called over her shoulder. "We'll talk when you come to the castle tomorrow morning." And she was relieved when Russell's smile didn't waver.

As they walked up the steps to the diner's entrance, she spoke in a low undertone to Duncan. "You were rude to him. He's doing an article on the castle that could be instrumental in building Adair's and Vi's destination wedding business."

"Until we figure out exactly what's going on here, you are not having drinks and dinner with a stranger."

She shot him a sideways glance. "I would have insisted that you come along. And one of the perks of on-demand sex is that there's no reason to feel jealous."

"Well, as you so correctly pointed out in the woods, this sex-on-demand thing isn't as simple as it seems on the surface. We clearly don't have the hang of it yet, so we'll just have to keep practicing."

"You *are* jealous." The idea of that thrilled her to the bone. It made the nerves that had been growing tighter in her stomach ease.

With his hand on the doorknob, all Duncan said was, "Ready for this?"

"Yes."

He pushed through the doors. Piper immediately noticed the scent of fried onions, grilling meat and coffee, and the sounds of an old-fashioned jukebox pumping out country music. In the kitchen, Edie, with her cloud of tightly curled red hair and a pair of reading glasses perched low on her nose, turned a welcoming wave into a thumbs-up gesture before she turned back to flip a burger high in the air. There was a smattering of applause from the customers at the counter.

"Corner booth to your right," Duncan murmured before he steered her in that direction. The booths surrounding it were empty, partly due to the fact that at two-thirty, the lunch rush was over and partly due to the "Reserved" signs on the tables.

Piper spotted Sheriff Morris Skinner first. His hair had gotten a bit thinner and grayer, his midsection a little thicker since she'd seen him last, but the smile was the same. The other man with a smaller build sat across from him. Piper couldn't prevent the knot of nerves from tightening again in her stomach.

When they reached the booth, Duncan slid in beside Patrick Lightman and she took the space opposite beside the sheriff. It was such a smooth maneuver, boxing in Lightman and putting her across from him— Piper couldn't help but wonder if Duncan and Skinner had planned it out in advance. Or perhaps it was bred into the gene pool of men who had been born to protect and serve.

Then she pushed the errant thought away and focused her entire attention on Patrick Lightman.

"Ms. MacPherson, I'm so happy to make your acquaintance." He stretched out a hand.

Skinner gripped Lightman's wrist and set it back down on the table. "Hands to yourself. That was part of our agreement."

"Sorry." Lightman kept his eyes steady on Piper's.

They were intense and very blue. And they'd registered no surprise at Duncan's appearance. Since she'd taken her seat, he hadn't looked at anyone but her.

"Why exactly did you want to meet with me, Mr. Lightman?"

A thin smile curved his lips but didn't reach his eyes. "I wanted to thank you."

If he was hoping for a "you're welcome," he was plumb out of luck. In the silence, Piper continued to study him. The man looked just as he had in his photos and in the shots of him that the press had captured during his trial, except now he wasn't wearing glasses. In his late thirties, he was five-foot-eight or so, with the wiry and toned build of a jockey. Sandy brown hair fell in bangs over his forehead, and his face was on the pudgy side. If she'd passed him on the street, she wouldn't have given him a second look.

During the trial he'd worn black-framed glasses. They'd emphasized the nerdy, geek aura that Lightman exuded even now. Something tugged at the edge of her memory.

"Where are your glasses?" she asked.

He patted a hand on the pocket of his jacket. "I don't need them for everything."

"You didn't make a trip all the way up here just to say thank you," Skinner prompted.

Lightman's gaze never wavered from Piper's. "You've saved my life, and I thought I might return the favor."

"Are you saying her life is in danger?" Skinner's tone was mild, but Piper could feel the tension in his body.

"Whoever staged that little scene in your apartment doesn't wish you well, Piper."

His use of her first name sent a cold sliver of fear down her spine. Piper ignored it. "I know you didn't stage it."

"I may be able to help you identify who did."

"How?" Skinner asked.

"He's also been stalking me." Lightman shifted his gaze to the sheriff for the first time. "I recognized him. I'm going to reach into my pocket. You know I'm not armed."

Skinner nodded. "Go ahead."

Lightman pulled out his cell phone, a smartphone with a good-size screen, and placed it at the far end of the table. "I happened to have shot this little video clip."

He carefully pulled out his glasses and put them on. This close, Piper could see a designer logo on the side of the frames.

Out of the corner of her eye, she saw that Edie was polishing the nearby corner and no doubt picking up every word of their conversation. A couple of customers at the counter were also within earshot, not that they gave any indication they were eavesdropping. The jukebox had switched from Shania Twain to Katy Perry.

Reaching out, Lightman pressed something that set the video on the cell phone screen in motion. Piper immediately recognized the street in Georgetown where she routinely took her run. Just as she calculated that he must have shot it from the coffee shop two buildings down from her alley, she saw herself appear and head up the street.

"You were there," she said, forcing her voice to be steady as she tamped down on another sliver of fear. "You were watching me. Why?"

"You saved my life," he said. "The Macks family has been harassing me ever since I got out of jail. Have you seen them on TV? And they're bothering my friend Abe. I figured it was only a matter of time before they got around to you. You were the one who saved me, so I was keeping an eye out for you. I pay my debts."

"How did you know Ms. MacPherson was responsible for your release?" Duncan asked.

"Abe told me. Watch. This is the important part," Lightman said.

And it was. She was barely out of the picture frame when a figure appeared on the sidewalk wearing jeans and a hooded sweatshirt and carrying a shopping bag. He moved quickly, disappearing into the alleyway she'd just jogged out of. The video followed his progress as he hurriedly climbed the steps that led to her apartment. Then it lingered as the man inserted a key and stepped through the door.

"That's the same person I've seen walking up and down my street," Lightman said. "And he'll follow me if I let him."

"Do you know who it is?" Duncan asked.

"No. Sorry, but I didn't get a clear shot of his face when he came out." To prove his point, he swiped a finger across the cell phone and they watched the man hurry down the stairs, pause to toss a shopping bag into a Dumpster and then jog up the street in the same direction Piper had taken. Once again, the hood prevented a clear view of his features.

When the screen went blank, Piper met Duncan's eyes. She could tell he was thinking the same thing she was. The person they'd spotted running on the beach below the caves had also been wearing a hooded sweatshirt. Coincidence?

Piper shifted her gaze to Lightman. "What else can you tell us about him?"

Over the top of his glasses, he met her eyes. "He's about five feet, ten inches, slender build, weighs about a hundred and thirty. My guess is that it's Suzanne Macks's brother, Sid."

"You must have followed him. Where did he go?" Duncan asked.

"He used the Metro. I don't." Lightman shuddered slightly. "Too crowded. Too many germs."

"How long was he in the apartment?" Duncan asked.

"Five minutes or so." His eyes remained steady on Piper's. "After he left, I went up to check and to see what he'd done."

Lightman pressed something on his cell. More video followed, but Piper would have sworn that it wasn't the same one that the TV stations had played and replayed. The angle was different, and it remained totally focused on the sheet with its display of rose petals.

When the screen went blank again, Sheriff Skinner

spoke. "Why didn't you come forward and give those video clips to the D.C. police?"

"They wouldn't have paid me any heed. They didn't do anything when I complained about the Macks family—or about the guy watching my apartment. So I decided to bring them directly to Ms. MacPherson. I figured they'd listen to her."

"Would you send those video clips to my cell right now?" Skinner took out a card and pushed it toward Lightman, then waited for the man to push the buttons.

"Thanks," Skinner said when the transmission was completed. "I'll see they get to the police in D.C. How did you know where to find Ms. MacPherson?"

"Abe's office told me she was out of town for a few days, and I figured she'd probably come up here. It was a lucky guess."

"Thank you for your help," Piper said as Duncan slid out of his side of the booth. "I appreciate your making such a long trip from D.C. Have a safe journey back."

"Oh, I'm not leaving Glen Loch." Lightman took his glasses off, replaced them in his pocket and picked up his cell phone. "Didn't the sheriff tell you? I'm staying at a charming bed-and-breakfast, the Eagle's Nest." He kept his eyes on her as he slid out of the booth. "Till we meet again."

Piper absolutely hated the fact that she had to suppress a shudder. Duncan remained standing until Lightman had exited through the diner's doors. The instant he sat down again, he took her hand in his and gave it a squeeze.

Edie hurried over and delivered three mugs of coffee. "What a creep. These are on the house. If I had my way, I'd have put something stronger than coffee in his." She dropped a hand on Piper's shoulder and gave it a squeeze. "Don't you worry. We'll keep an eye on him."

"She will, too," Skinner said. "As will I. Are you buying his story?"

Duncan answered first. "Not entirely. He's not telling us everything he knows. And Sid Macks has an airtight alibi for the time Lightman was shooting that video."

"I don't believe Macks staged the scene in my apartment," Piper said. Then she told Skinner about the two vases of flowers that had been delivered and the message on the second one.

"He used the exact words that were on the third card," Duncan said.

"But if he's the guy behind all this, he's breaking pattern," Piper said.

"And who's the guy in the hoodie?" Skinner shifted his gaze out the window to where Lightman had settled himself on a park bench. "I'll keep my eye on him. While we've been chatting, my deputy Tim has been checking out Lightman's room at the Eagle's Nest. It'll be wired by the time he's finished. Other than that, my hands are tied. Lightman's a free man."

"Thanks to me," Piper said.

Duncan took her hands and held them so tight, Piper was afraid he was stopping the blood. Startled, she met his eyes and she saw anger, this time hot enough to nearly singe her skin.

"He wasn't hanging out over at your apartment to say thank-you. My theory is he was stalking you and ran into some competition. I want to get you away from here. Now."

Before she could even open her mouth, Skinner

spoke in a voice that didn't carry. "Not the place to make a scene."

He was right. And she and Duncan could hardly take the discussion outside when Lightman had decided to sit down on a park bench across the street and enjoy the view of the lake. Still, Piper had to bite down hard on her tongue. It gave her some satisfaction to see that Duncan was struggling also.

When he spoke, it was in a very low tone. "A serial killer has taken a fancy to you. He's followed you up here and he intends to stay."

She could see the argument he was making. She did fit the description of the RPK's victims. And the fact that Lightman had taken pictures of her the day before made her skin crawl. But she couldn't run. Where could she go?

Pitching her voice very low, she asked, "What if he's telling the truth?" Impatience flickered across Duncan's features, but he eased the pressure on her fingers enough for her to turn them and grip his. "Or at least a partial truth. Why would he pick me as his next victim? He'd have the spotlight turned on him full force and he'd lose his good friend Abe as his defense attorney."

"Go on," Duncan said. He was listening now.

"Even if he was stalking me, he isn't anymore. If he were, why seek the spotlight like this? Why come all the way up here, contact the sheriff and offer to turn over those video clips? That isn't the RPK's profile. He's gotten away with what he has because he stays in the background. No one ever sees him. If I were to end up on a sheet with rose petals strewn over me now, he'd be the prime suspect."

"She's making sense," Skinner said.

Duncan was aware of that. She was making perfect

sense. And she was doing what he should be doing—getting into Lightman's head and thinking the way he was thinking. The RPK was very smart, and while he might have been tempted by the idea of targeting Piper, might even have been considering it, he wouldn't have come up here, notified the sheriff and moved into the bed-and-breakfast. Would he? Duncan wasn't sure. Usually, he was. "He was on your street, watching your apartment, yesterday morning."

"Maybe out of concern. I did help to get him out of jail. The crazy thing is he might even be trying to do the white knight thing," Piper said.

Duncan's lips almost curved. "Let's not get carried away." He glanced at the sheriff. "Even when we were kids, Piper never liked to play the role of damsel in distress. White knights riding to the rescue are not her thing."

He admired that about her, he thought as he studied her. It was part of what had always attracted him. He also liked the way her mind had zeroed in on the facts and then arranged them into a persuasive argument. He could see what she was saying about Lightman as clearly as she did. The problem was that his emotions were blurring everything. If he wanted to keep her safe, he had to keep his mind as focused as hers was.

He turned to Skinner. "Can you verify Lightman's whereabouts shortly after noon?"

"No. My first contact with him was just before I called you at about one-forty-five, give or take a few minutes. That was right after he made his request for a meeting. I can see when he checked in at the Eagle's Nest."

"Do that."

The sheriff made a quick call and got the answer.

"Ada says he checked in at one-fifteen, took his bag up to the room and then asked for directions to my office. Why do you want to know?"

He told the sheriff about their adventure and their discovery in the caves.

At the end of it, Skinner said, "So another piece of Eleanor Campbell MacPherson's dowry has surfaced. I assume you've secured it."

"It's in the Fort Knox-quality safe that Cam had installed," Duncan said.

Skinner took a sip of coffee. "And it could have been Lightman who followed you into the caves. But you say the person you saw was wearing a hooded sweatshirt. I know they're pretty common apparel, but could it have been the guy Lightman filmed going into Piper's apartment?"

"Both are possibilities. The hooded sweatshirt guy could have taken a lucky guess and followed her up here just as Lightman did," Duncan admitted as he cursed himself silently. The problem was that he hadn't been thinking straight since Piper had walked into her apartment yesterday morning. If he had, he might have found a safer place to take her. Although where that might be, he didn't know.

"Or the person who followed us into the cave could be the person Cam believed was paying regular visits to the library," Piper said, then explained what she and Duncan had theorized about in the woods.

"Or someone new," Skinner mused. "The Stuart Sapphires have brought fortune hunters out of the woodwork before. And the news that you've discovered a second earring will leak out soon enough." He glanced around the diner. "Anything that's said in this place goes viral almost immediately."

"So we're back to a whole cornucopia of suspects. Happy thought," Piper said.

"Plus, there are those people from *Architectural Digest* planning on their photo shoot tomorrow." At Duncan's raised brows, Skinner shrugged. "The town has been buzzing about it for weeks. They're staying at the same bed-and-breakfast as our friend Lightman. The woman left early with her camera to take location shots around the lake. I can check on that. The man has been exploring the village, talking to the locals, visiting the library. He's even visited the college. When do you expect Vi and Daryl Garnett to be back?"

"Roughly around dinnertime," Duncan said. "They're going to leave Albany right after Vi's presentation winds up."

"I told Vi I'd stop by tomorrow for the photo shoot. But I could send someone out to the castle until they arrive tonight," Skinner offered.

"I think we'll be fine until the CIA arrives." Duncan offered his hand to the sheriff and then rose. "Thanks for your help—and for the information."

Lightman was still sitting on the park bench taking in the view when they stepped out of the diner.

"I'd still like to get you away from here," Duncan murmured as he escorted her to the car and opened the door.

Lightman turned, beamed a smile and waved.

Stifling the sick surge in her stomach, Piper muttered as she slid into her seat and clenched her fists in her lap. "There's a part of me that wants to run. But running never solves anything."

She was right, he thought, as he joined her in the car. That's what his mother and A. D. MacPherson had done after that summer when they'd first met. They'd fallen in love, then they'd run away from it and waited for a decade to act on what they'd felt.

"Let's go back to the castle and take a closer look at those files," Piper said. "I helped let that monster out and I'm going to put him back behind bars."

Duncan took one of her clenched fists in his hand, raised it to his lips and kissed it. "*We're* going to put him back behind bars."

10

STRETCHED OUT FULL LENGTH ON one of the leather sofas in the library, Piper slept with the same focused intensity that she worked. Duncan leaned back in his chair and watched her, fascinated. A short time earlier, he'd opened the sliding doors to the terrace to alleviate some of the stuffiness of the room, and the only sounds that interrupted the silence were the breeze stirring the pines and the occasional call of a bird. Alba slept in the one remaining patch of sunlight she could find near the open doors.

He and Piper had worked for nearly two hours on the RPK files before she'd taken one to the sofa and stretched out with it. For about five minutes she'd lain on her stomach, propping herself up with her elbows. Then her head had simply fallen onto the report she'd been reading and she'd dropped into sleep as abruptly and thoroughly as an infant.

She hadn't moved an inch since. It was little wonder that she was exhausted. They'd had quite a couple of days. And though they hadn't discovered anything yet in the files, they'd each made their way through two more boxes.

Better than that, he'd gotten a feeling that they were going to find something in them. He'd been through the files before, of course. He'd started on them the day that the verdict had been handed down on Lightman's appeal. But he hadn't had even a trace of a feeling then.

What was different now was that he was working with Piper. And to his surprise, he was enjoying it. Bouncing ideas off her and talking about them was nearly as exciting as making love to her.

He'd always preferred to work alone. Even his brothers had been aware of that. During those times when he'd gone into the field, he'd had partners; that was standard protocol. But in his office at Quantico, he usually kept the door closed because he didn't like interruptions or idle chatter.

From the time they'd reentered the library, Piper had offered neither. Instead, she'd seemed as totally absorbed in the work as he. Whatever his motivations, Patrick Lightman had made a mistake by taking a personal interest in Piper. For a moment, Duncan's mind flashed to those seconds in the diner when Lightman had been playing the video clip, and he freed the anger that he worked hard to keep on a very tight leash.

He'd been right about the fact that Lightman had been stalking Piper. But she may have been right about the reason. Maybe in a twisted way, he did want to protect her. Maybe.

More than likely, Lightman was jealous that someone else was stalking her and had decided to get even. Either way, the man was going down. He shifted his eyes to the boxes of files. The answer was in them somewhere, and she was going to lead him to it the same way she'd led him to the sapphire earring.

But where else was she going to lead them both?

She'd made clear what she wanted. Simple, uncomplicated, no-strings sex—anytime, anyplace. The idea certainly held appeal. And it had held a lot of appeal for him in the past. Relationships demanded time. They also demanded risks, ones he'd studiously avoided. His mother had taken that risk. He believed that she'd truly loved his father, and when she'd had to face and accept the fact that he'd never loved her or his sons, he'd seen the price she'd had to pay. Then he'd watched her spend a great deal of her life trying to avoid taking that risk again.

So that summer, when he and his brothers were ten, she'd agreed to have a summer romance with A.D. Whatever one called it—a summer romance, a fling, an affair or no-strings sex on demand, the concept hadn't changed. Keep it simple.

The smart thing to do was to play it Piper's way and do just that. He could go to her right now and join her on that couch. In minutes, seconds even, he could wake her and arouse her. He could taste her and experience the thrill, the incredible generosity of her response, and he could sink into her and lose himself in her again. Just the thought of it was enough to have everything in him hardening. Yearning. They could be moving together in that lightning-fast rhythm that he could only create with her. The thought of it had him aching.

He wanted to touch her. He couldn't seem to get enough of simply running his hands over her skin. Softly and slowly. He imagined tracing that delicate cheekbone with his fingers, then the strong line of her jaw. In his mind, he already smelled the faint scent of summer flowers in her hair. Next he'd explore the slender line of her neck, then her collarbone and that surprisingly muscled arm. Those amber eyes would be open by then. He pictured them golden and clouded with sleep, watched them focus and darken as he turned her, straddled her on the couch, and continued to touch her.

As the images grew more and more clear in his mind, his blood began to pound and the ache inside of him intensified. She would reach for him, eager to make her own demands. That much he knew. So he'd capture those slender wrists, hold them over her head, and continue to savor the slow heating of her skin and the husky sound of her voice as she said his name.

He clamped his fingers on the arms of the chair as his mind flashed to another scenario. He imagined freeing her hands and lowering his mouth to hers. He was half out of his chair when his cell phone vibrated in his pocket. He slipped quietly through the sliding glass doors to the terrace. A quick glance at the caller ID told him it was his brother Cam.

"Problem or favor?" Duncan asked.

"Question. When were you going to get around to telling me that you found the second sapphire earring?"

Shit, Duncan thought. Connecting the dots in his head, he remembered that he'd told Daryl, and Piper had relayed the news to Vi. Obviously, one of them had passed the news along.

"Vi told Adair you and Piper found the earring in one of the caves where I killed you and Reid when we were playing pirates."

"The way I remember it, I killed *you* several times."

Cam laughed. "Funny, but I don't remember it that way. And Adair will back me up."

"Piper has a pretty accurate memory of what actually went on in those caves," he warned. "In fact, she found a third cave that you and I and Reid missed. That's where we found the second sapphire earring."

"A third cave. No shit. But you still haven't answered my question. Why am I hearing about all of this secondhand? Wasn't I the one who had the brilliant idea you should go up there?"

Duncan glanced back through the glass at Piper. "I've been a little busy." So busy that he'd forgotten to phone his brother about the discovery of a priceless earring.

"With Piper. I understand. Daryl filled me in on her situation and the fact that someone followed you into the caves. Adair's worried."

Duncan believed that. He also knew his brother's concern was the real reason for the phone call. "Daryl doesn't know yet about the latest development. Neither does Vi." He filled Cam in on Patrick Lightman's appearance in the village of Glen Loch.

"So you've got a mysterious guy in a hoodie sending threatening notes and vases of roses to Piper in D.C., someone else following you into our cave at the castle, a person who may or may not have been paying nocturnal visits to the library until we upped the security, and now a serial killer has joined the party."

Plus, he had this no-strings sex-on-demand relationship going on with Piper. Which was obviously distracting him. But what Duncan said was, "Those are the highlights."

"And here I thought that it might be Piper who was keeping you so preoccupied."

Duncan frowned. One of the plagues of growing up with brothers was that they could read you very well.

"Those secret sexual fantasies the sisters buried in that metal box can keep you busy," Cam said.

Duncan waited a beat before he took the bait. "Secret sexual fantasies?"

"Piper didn't mention them yet?"

"No." Duncan sat down on the stone wall that bordered the terrace and kept his gaze on Piper.

"Adair didn't tell me about what was in the box, either," Cam said. "But my curiosity got the best of me."

Duncan had to laugh. "There's a surprise."

"Hey, I'm trying to do you a favor here. I figure I owe you one after I asked you to bring that reluctant bridegroom back from Montana. And I like to pay my debts."

"I'm all ears."

"From the time they were little, Adair, Piper and Nell wrote down their private thoughts on paper, locked them in a metal box and buried that box beneath some of the stones in the arch so they could tap into the power of the legend."

"Vi mentioned that to me," Duncan said. "Not a bad plan."

"It gets better. On the night that our mother married A.D., they drank a little champagne and decided to write down their most secret fantasies. Sexual ones. And they put them into the box and tucked them back into the stones."

"Adair told you all of this?" Duncan asked.

"Not at first." Cam cleared his throat. "She was showing me where she and Vi found the first earring and we accidentally dug out the box. I was naturally curious, and when she ran off with the thing, I looked into the matter."

"What good CIA agent wouldn't?"

"Exactly. First chance I got, I read all of them. I knew which one was Adair's right away. And brother to brother, I'll give you a hint that might help you to identify Piper's. To ensure privacy, they each wrote their fantasies down on different colored paper. Adair's are the yellow ones. So you have a fifty-fifty chance that Piper's fantasy is written on either the blue or the pink paper. I'm thinking that a top-notch FBI profiler like you should be able to figure it out."

"Just where is this metal box?"

"Still buried in the stone arch. Adair wanted her sisters to still have the power working for them. Look for loose stones at the base about two feet in on the right. At the very least, they make very interesting reading," Cam prodded. "If you have the time."

Duncan continued to study Piper's prone form on the couch. She was still out for the count, and a quick glance at his watch told him that Vi and Daryl wouldn't arrive for another couple of hours. The timing was perfect.

What he said to Cam was, "Before I let you go, what have you found out on your end about Eleanor Campbell and Angus One and their elopement from Scotland? Russell Arbogast, the senior editor from *Architectural Digest,* says that he's seen the original stone arch on the Campbell family's estate."

"I'm looking at it right now. A.D. is painting it. Thanks to Mom's meticulous research, we're visiting the ancestral home of the Campbells, and she's even gotten the current owners to let her do some research in their library. The bad news is that about a hundred years ago, there was a fire. Many of the books were destroyed. But if there's something on this end about Eleanor's dowry, Mom'll track it down. In the meantime, enjoy your reading."

That was exactly what he intended to do, Duncan

decided as he disconnected the call. Moving quietly through the sliding doors, he closed them, turned on the security system and activated the cameras.

When Alba lifted her head, Duncan signaled her to stay and retrieved his reading glasses from the desk. Then he let himself out into the hallway and locked that door also.

PIPER SURFACED SLOWLY, drifting in that dreamy zone between waking and sleeping while sensations penetrated one by one: a low sound she couldn't quite nail down, the soft press of leather beneath her legs, something with an edge to it poking into her cheek. And a prickling at the back of her neck.

The prickling grew stronger. Someone watching her? The sound came again.

A growl.

Opening her eyes, she fought through a moment of disorientation. The library. She'd been working with Duncan and she must have dozed off. As she rubbed the back of her neck, she shifted her gaze to the desk where he'd been working earlier.

Gone. She didn't have to even glance around to see if he was somewhere else in the room. She would have sensed his presence, felt that low humming in her blood. Instead, she felt a pang so sharp, she had to rub the heel of her hand against her chest to ease it. Disappointment that he was gone?

And if Duncan wasn't here, whose eyes had she felt?

The growl sounded again, starting low and building into an insistent bark. Alba. The dog stood on her hind legs, pawing at the glass doors that led outside. Piper sprang up from the couch and ran to join her. Stroking the dog's head, she focused on the stretch of lawn beyond the low terrace wall. A storage shed sat near the line of trees that bordered the castle on this side. The doors were closed. To the left, she could just see the bright blue of the lake and the dark clouds that had formed on the opposite shore. To the right, more trees.

No one in sight.

Alba dropped to all fours and growled again.

"I agree, girl," Piper said as she stroked the dog's head. Someone had been at these doors looking in.

And that's when she saw them. She'd been so intent on looking at the space beyond the terrace that her gaze had shot right over the flagstones. Slivers of fear shot up her spine.

Red rose petals, hundreds of them, lay strewn across a white sheet. It looked as if it had been raining blood. She tried the door and found it locked. The security light on the pad was blinking. Duncan must have engaged it before he'd left. The cameras would have caught whoever had done this. She wouldn't do much about it now, any case. And she'd be damned if she'd let this creep scare her.

Alba growled again. Piper patted her head. The dog wanted to give chase.

"Me, too," she murmured. "But it wouldn't be smart. That's probably just what they want." And if Duncan hadn't slowed her down enough so she had to think, she might be out there right now.

A faint rumble of thunder sounded in the distance.

Where was he anyway? This time the fear was sharper. Had he seen the person and given chase himself? "Duncan?"

Whirling from the window, she raced the length of the library and opened the door to the hallway. "Duncan?"

No answer.

Once Alba joined her, she locked the library door and hurried to the kitchen. But she knew he wouldn't be there even before she entered. He would have answered. Turning on a dime, she ran back down the hall that led to the large foyer, calling his name again.

The only answer was Alba's bell as she followed.

At the foot of the stairs, Piper made herself stop. Pressing a hand to her chest, she took a deep breath. Silly to panic. What in the world was the matter with her? Duncan was a smart man. Not only that, he was an FBI agent. She thought of his big gun. He could handle himself.

But there was that person who'd followed them into the cave that morning. And there was Patrick Lightman, who seemed to have a knack for slipping away from surveillance any time he felt like it.

Squaring her shoulders, she climbed onto the first step. She'd just search the castle, room by room, until she found him. Alba whined and she turned to see the dog standing at one of the glass windows that framed the front door. When she got there, she scanned what she could see of the yard. The drive was empty.

Alba whined again.

Piper spotted Duncan then. Because her view was partially blocked by the garden, she could only see the side of his face and his shoulder. He was in the stone arch. Even as she watched, he raised a hand to brush it through his hair.

And he was wearing his glasses. Of course. Maybe he'd needed a change of scene. He'd probably taken a file out there to read. Maybe he was thinking the power of the legend would give him some insights.

"He's fine," she assured Alba. The degree of relief

she was feeling was ridiculous. And telling. It wasn't just that for a couple of minutes she'd been afraid for him. When she'd woken up in the library and found him gone, she'd actually missed him.

"No, no, no." Alba's bell jingled and Piper glanced down to see the dog was looking at her strangely. "I'm not talking to you." She paced to the stairs and back. "It's just the stress. It's been a long day. Starting with digging that box out of the stones and refreshing my mind about that sexual fantasy I wrote with Duncan in mind."

Alba had stretched out on the floor and tilted her head to one side.

"So, I decided why not? On-demand sex is simple, uncomplicated. The perfect solution to the fact that I couldn't stop thinking about getting my hands on him. And I was nineteen when I thought it up."

When she paused, Alba just looked at her.

"Okay, so I'm older now and supposedly wiser, and it still seemed like the perfect solution this morning. Maybe it would have been if it hadn't been for the person who followed us into the cave or the fact that Patrick Lightman, aka the RPK, has decided to be my BFF."

Alba was looking at her as if she were taking in every word.

Piper sank onto the floor in front of her. "It still is a good solution. I want him. He wants me. All I have to do is keep the complicated stuff in a bottle."

Closing her eyes, she pictured the bottle. Then she imagined the words that described what she'd been feeling in the library. Fear. That funny kind of emptiness. That incredible and scary yearning. And…she felt her heart take a little bounce. Okay—panic, too.

Those were the emotions that she could put a name to when she'd woken up alone. In her mind, she did what she could to separate each word into letters and imagined them disappearing into the bottle. Then she jammed the cork in.

"There." She opened her eyes and looked into Alba's. Leaning forward, she hugged the dog. "You're a good listener." She rose to her feet and reached for the door handle. "And now that I've sorted everything out, I'm in the mood for some sex on demand."

Thunder rumbled again.

_11_

DUNCAN HAD SPENT MOST OF HIS adult career getting into other people's heads. He was good at it. He enjoyed it. But he didn't think he'd ever looked forward to doing it quite this much. The metal box had been right where Cam had said it would be—a couple of feet into the stone arch on the right. No CIA or FBI skills involved. The stones were loose, as if they'd been recently replaced in a hurry.

Had Piper dug out the box? Was that why she'd paid that early morning visit to the stone arch?

It was the size of a cigar box, but sturdy. The small padlock hadn't even been fully closed. The compartments inside were filled with scraps of paper in three colors, just as Cam had said, and they all seemed to be folded. That argued that, in spite of the fact the sisters had shared the box, they'd valued each other's privacy.

A pang of guilt assaulted him, but it wasn't enough to make him close the box. If Piper had a fantasy that she'd buried in the stones, he wanted to know what it was. More, he wanted to fulfill it.

He took Cam's word that the yellow paper was

Adair's. And pink seemed to fit Nell with her blond curls and blue eyes. She'd even worn a pink dress on the day that their parents had wed.

And Piper was the middle sister; logically, she would choose or be assigned the middle section of the box. He assumed the fantasies the girls had penned were on the larger sheets of paper that lay on the top of the compartments. To test his theory, he lifted the blue one and selected one of the smaller scraps of folded paper beneath it.

I want to win the spelling bee on Friday.

A noble ambition, but not telling. He could imagine any one of the MacPherson girls being that competitive. Digging deeper, he selected another one.

One day I want to clerk on the Supreme Court.

Bingo, he thought. That could only be Piper. Then because he couldn't help himself, he opened a few more. The wish to master long division made him smile. The wish that she would one day become a black belt fascinated him. Had she achieved it? And how many other things didn't he know about her dreams and ambitions?

A lot, he thought as he stared at how crammed her compartment was. Not that her sisters were slackers. His admiration for the MacPherson sisters grew. There was a lot of academic research to support the fact that simply writing down one's goals dramatically increased the odds of achieving them. Kudos to the girls for tapping into that power, as well as whatever extra power the stone arch possessed because of the legend.

Inspired, he pulled out a pen, and using the back of Piper's wish to win a spelling bee, he wrote: "Keep Piper and the other MacPhersons safe." Then he folded it and buried the slip of paper beneath the others.

Only then did he pick up the folded blue sheets of paper on the top of the center compartment. "My Sexual Fantasy: Sex on Demand."

He skimmed the first page. It presented various settings and scenarios for making love, each one spur of the moment. On a deserted beach with the waves pounding on the shore, in a limo, on a coffee table, on a bathroom counter. There were more on the second page—some of which went beyond his own experience. He had to admit, he'd never made love to a woman in a phone booth—but then seven years had passed since this had been written and phone booths were hard to find. By the time he'd finished the last one, he'd had to use the sheets of paper to fan himself.

Each scene illustrated the excitement and convenience of sex on demand with someone you trusted. A buddy. At least one could even have been "monkey sex," he supposed. But the writer hadn't used those specific words. Still, they all fit the description she'd given him when she'd made her argument in the library.

Besides making him want to go back to the library and wake her up, reading the pages had also left a bitter coppery taste in his mouth. Who had she imagined doing all these things with?

As he'd read them, he'd thought only of her. And he wanted her again. Right now.

"You...you jerk."

He turned and found himself staring at Piper. Her image was blurred because of his reading glasses. And it wasn't Diana he thought of as he removed the glasses and set them aside. She looked like one of the Furies from one of those Greek tragedies that always ended badly.

The flash of lightning over the lake strengthened the illusion.

"You broke into our box."

He was surprised that more lightning didn't shoot out from the accusing finger she pointed at him.

"And you read them?"

Not only read them, but he'd been too caught up in them to hear her approach.

"You read them." It wasn't a question this time. And the tone was enough to have him getting to his feet. Growing up with three brothers, he'd learned there were serious disadvantages to being a sitting target.

"How did you know about them? Who told you?"

"Cam." He hated to betray a brother, but Cam was an ocean away and desperate situations called for desperate measures. He took a cautious step forward.

"Not so fast," she said. "You…you just put them all back where you found them. Right now."

Without another word, Duncan did as she asked. Keeping quiet had gotten him out of plenty of scrapes as a child. Letting Reid and Cam do all the talking had focused his mother's attention on them. Not that he'd gotten off scot-free—but a strategic silence had often lessened the punishment his mother had meted out.

He took his time, sliding the metal box back into its niche, then shoving the stones back in place. He figured that with each passing second her temper had to be cooling. That was what had happened with his mother.

"Now, step out here and fight like a man."

One look told him her temper hadn't cooled one degree. She was crouched, arms bent, hands flexed in a stance that he knew all too well. As she stood there waiting, several things flashed into his mind—*I don't want to hurt you* being the first. He rejected it. Being condescending and sexist was only going to dig him deeper into the hole he'd dug.

Besides, he always liked to err on the side of caution. "What degree of black belt?" he asked.

"Fourth." The fact that she smiled when she said it sent a shaft of fire straight to his loins.

Still, his rational side kept him standing where he was. Now was the time to offer excuses, explanations. Except that he had none.

"I'd apologize," he said. "But it would be a lie." The temptation to read her fantasy had been irresistible. Every bit as irresistible as the outrageous temptation to take her on in a fight.

He sprang out of the arch to land lightly on his feet in a stance that matched hers. Clouds had rolled in overhead, darkening the sky, but he saw the excitement in her eyes—not fear or panic but an excitement that fueled his own.

"What degree are you?" she asked.

"We should be evenly matched." He partially blocked the first blow. Still, it sang up his arm to resonate in his shoulder. Then he had to shift quickly to prevent a well-aimed kick from connecting with his chin.

She was fast and agile. He kept his moves defensive as he tried to assess her strengths and weaknesses. Which were damned few, he decided, as her foot connected solidly enough with his hip to send him stumbling back a few steps. Admiration streamed through him along with the zing of pain.

Overhead, the thunder clapped loudly.

He was going to have to go on the offensive. Or he might just end up on his back with her foot on his throat. The next kick, which sailed past his guard and into his rib cage, confirmed his decision.

After five sweaty minutes, he was breathing hard and she seemed to be just hitting her stride. The rain had begun to fall in needlelike pellets. They ignored it. He'd been absolutely correct in his prediction that they'd be evenly matched. Except that he was taller, heavier, and his reach was longer. He might even have used one of his advantages if he hadn't decided that fighting with her was almost as absorbing and enjoyable as making love with her. Then without warning, she slipped close enough to hook her foot behind his and flip him to the ground. He landed hard on his backside just inside the stone arch.

The instant before her foot came down on his throat, he grabbed her ankle and jerked her down on top of him. Then he rolled so that she was trapped beneath him. To his surprise, he found the struggle wasn't over. He had to use his full weight to keep her there as he pinned her hands above her head. And thanks to a bright flash of lightning, he read the intent in those golden eyes and shifted out of the way just in time to prevent her knee from connecting with his groin.

For seconds, neither of them moved. He was winded. A first for him. And she wasn't done. The heat of battle was still strong in her eyes. In the dim light, they gleamed at him as tawny and challenging as those of Alice's Cheshire cat. Duncan felt his heart go into free fall, and it seemed to be the most natural thing in the world to lower his mouth to hers. The instant their lips met, he felt what he'd known from the first. She was right for him. Just simply right.

He wanted to show her that there was lovemaking beyond what she'd described in her fantasies. And he wanted more from her than convenient buddy sex. So for both of them, he kept the pressure of the kiss light, letting his lips toy with hers, then drawing back just far enough to feather kisses along her jaw to her ear. The rain was loud now, pounding on the stones overhead and pouring in a thick sheet over both entrances to the arch. He couldn't hear her sigh above the noise, but he felt the quick expulsion of breath against his cheek and the beat of her pulse beneath his lips.

Then he returned to her mouth, nibbling first, then slipping his tongue in to taste. Her flavor was different, warm instead of hot, and as sweet as melting ice cream on a hot summer day. Unable to resist, he deepened the kiss, degree by degree, pulling them both under. His reward came slowly as he felt the tension drain slowly out of her. She gave him what she hadn't offered, even at the end of their fight. Pliancy and surrender. And he was utterly seduced.

DUNCAN. THAT WAS THE ONLY WORD she could form in her mind as his mouth toyed with hers. Her mind had emptied and filled with him. No one had ever kissed her like this, as if he had hours and hours to spend and intended to do just that. With his mouth alone, he weakened her, drained her and sent her floating. Pleasure ran through her like a slow-moving river that penetrated deeper and deeper into her system with each passing second.

He spoke at her ear. "Let go, Piper. Let go."

The echo of the words whispered through her head, and she did just what he asked. How could she not?

He released her wrists and began to touch her then, skimming his fingers down her arms, lingering at the curve of her elbow, then tracing her shoulders. He undressed her slowly, too, easing her shirt off, then drawing her shorts down, touching and tasting each inch of

her that he uncovered. No part of her was ignored. Her
nipples tingled from the brush of his fingers, the nip of
his teeth. The back of her knees ached and the curve of
her ankles throbbed with the memory of his caresses.

While the storm raged outside, she could focus on
nothing but the slow, powerful one that he was so intent on building in her body. Each press of his fingers,
each stroke of his tongue left a bright foreshadowing
of the flash of lightning and the outrageous heat to
come. But for the moment, his tenderness forestalled
it, invading her, consuming her.

She was his. Only his.

The words swirled in a thick mist in her brain and
hammered in her heart. It was as if he was trying to
keep her just this way, trapped in pleasure. But he
seemed to want to give her more, take more using his
mouth and tongue alone to drive her to a climax.

The pleasure slammed into her like a bare-knuckled
punch, going beyond anything she'd ever imagined,
anything she'd thought she could endure. Shuddering,
she hungered for more.

He gave her more. And took more. In the arch of
the stone walls, she knew only him—the taste, the
scent, the feel of him. She would have given him anything he asked. Each time she thought he would have
to end it, he found a new way to send her up and over
a new crest.

"More."

He drew her up then so that they were kneeling,
body to body, eye to eye. Still gripping her shoulders,
he mouthed the words, "I want more. I want everything."

The sound was inaudible above the noise of the
storm. But her eyes flashed as brilliant as the light-

ning, in triumph, in need. They worked together then to get rid of the barrier his clothes presented. Once he'd dealt with the condom, she eased him back onto the stones and straddled him. He reached for her to grip her hips, but she forestalled him by capturing his hands.

"Take more," she said as she straddled him, then lifted her hips and took him inside. "Take all of me."

His fingers gripped her hips, but trembled as she began to move. "Take everything."

Eyes locked, hands linked, they rode the storm.

AFTERWARD, THEY LAY TOGETHER beneath the stones. The fury of the storm had passed, but the rain continued to pour in sheets off both ends of the short tunnel. There was a part of Piper that wished they could stay right where they were, tucked away from the world. She knew that was a dangerous thought. It was always a mistake to wish for more than you could have.

But she was pretty sure the mistake had already been made.

Reality check, she lectured herself. And it was then that she remembered just how she and Duncan had ended up naked beneath the stone arch.

He'd invaded not only her privacy, but the privacy of her sisters, as well.

Raising her head, she looked him dead in the eye. "If you think that counts for make-up sex, you're wrong."

His burst of laughter filled the space.

She frowned and poked him in the shoulder. "Not funny."

"I know. Sorry." More laughter bubbled up. "I've just never tried to sort sex into so many different categories. Maybe it's a difference between the male and the female brain. I'm still trying to sort out buddy sex and monkey sex."

"Right. Now it's my turn to laugh."

To Duncan it sounded more like a snort.

"They've done studies on how many times men think about sex during the average day. With all the time your brains spend on it, don't tell me you don't sort the experience into categories."

He grinned at her. "I can't speak for all men, but I usually think along the lines of good, better, best." She was lying half on top of him, her arms folded. He took a lock of her hair and twisted it around his finger. "At this very minute, I'm thinking *now* or *later*."

"Later." She shoved herself to her knees, intending to start searching for clothes, but she cracked her head on the side of the stone arch.

And that was when reality hit her. "No. Oh, no."

Something in her tone had him sitting up and reaching for her. "You're hurt. Let me see."

"No." She pushed his hands away, picked up his shirt and shoved it at him. "My head's fine. Or I thought it was. But I can't seem to think straight when I'm around you. I definitely wasn't thinking." She waved a hand. "Do you have any idea what we just did?"

"I have a pretty good idea."

"You never should have come out here to read my fantasy. I never should have followed you. This was not supposed to happen. What we've been doing can't work. We have to stop right now."

Her voice was rising. She was rattled and he realized it was the first time he'd seen her that way. He put his hands on her shoulders, but she twisted out of his grip. "Why don't you explain what the problem is— and fill in the details?"

She waved a hand. "You kissed me and I kissed you back."

"I've kissed you before."

"Not *here*. We just kissed under the stones. We made love *here*. That was not supposed to happen. A sexual fantasy is one thing. A great thing. But I don't want to have anything to do with the legend and its power. And I certainly don't want to fall in love with someone. Do you?"

"No." The answer came out quickly. It was the truth. He didn't want to fall in love with anyone. Something tightened around his heart.

"Good." She placed a hand against her heart and rubbed it. "We're in agreement. What we're doing. It has to stop now."

And what if they couldn't stop it? What if it was already too late? What if he'd already fallen in love with her? There were things he wanted to say. But before he did, Duncan had to work them out in his own mind. What he said was what he knew for sure. "We'll figure out a solution, Piper. You're good at that, and so am I."

But Duncan was careful not to touch her as they gathered up their clothes and dressed. And when she handed him the reading glasses he'd set aside, she was careful that her hand didn't come in contact with his.

The rain had slowed, and while they'd been safe enough in the stone arch during the Adirondack monsoon they'd just experienced, he wanted to get her back in the castle. He had to agree with her insistence that they put a halt to what was happening between them—because he'd lost track of everything while they'd been making love.

And Piper's life was in danger.

When they were ready to leave the stone arch, the rain had stopped completely, and the early-evening sun was throwing long shadows across the garden. He figured that Daryl and Vi would be arriving soon.

The sound of gravel crunching had them both turning toward the driveway as a truck pulled to a stop in front of the castle doors. The sign on the door read Margie's Flowers. Duncan noted that the location was Glen Loch, New York.

He got a bad feeling then, and he kept Piper behind him as they walked toward the man who climbed out. Before they even reached him, he unloaded a vase of red roses.

"For Piper MacPherson," he said with a smile.

"Do you know who placed the order?" Duncan asked as Piper took the vase.

The man shook his head. "My wife took the order over the phone. They paid extra for a speedy delivery. Not that they had to. We're mighty grateful for the business that Miss Vi and Miss Adair are bringing in to all the merchants in Glen Loch." Then he nodded to both of them and climbed back into his truck.

"I can call Sheriff Skinner," Duncan said as he opened the door. "He might be able to get a phone number or trace the credit card."

Saying nothing, Piper set the vase on a table in the foyer as he locked the door and reset the alarm.

Duncan wanted to touch her, to simply run a hand down her arm, to tell her that she'd be safe. More than that, he wanted to pull her into his arms, to tell her… The problem was there was too much to tell her. And it wasn't the time.

Instead, he reached for the note on the vase of flowers and opened it. The message wasn't written on vellum, but it was clear.

TILL WE MEET AGAIN. AND WE WILL VERY SOON.

The words told him what he'd already known. Time was running out.

12

"THERE'S MORE," PIPER SAID. "And you're not going to like it."

That's what she'd said the moment that she'd looked up from the note. Then she'd led him into the library. And she'd been right. He didn't like it at all.

Duncan silently cursed himself as he stood next to her and studied the rose petals that had been strewn over the white sheet on the terrace outside the library. He'd contacted Skinner and Adrienne. Lightman had been in plain sight all afternoon—sitting on the park bench and taking in the view of the lake. Richard Stark-weather and Sid Macks were both still in D.C., their movements accounted for.

As he'd relayed the news to Piper, he'd wanted more than anything to simply pull her into his arms and hold her. But he didn't dare. Everything on the terrace had been pounded by the downpour, but even in the long shadows cast by the late afternoon sunlight, the wet rose petals looked like drops of blood.

And that could easily have been the case. It could have been Piper's blood he was looking at. He'd left her alone because his mind had been so full of her, so obsessed with her, that he'd gone out to the stone arch to find out what her secret fantasy had been when she was nineteen.

Idiot. He cursed himself again. No woman had even come close to turning him into one before. If he was going to keep her safe, it had to stop.

About fifteen feet separated the scene he was studying from the couch where he'd left her sleeping. And she'd been there alone when the psycho had set up the little tableau for her. A mix of emotions assaulted him as he stood there, imagining what she might have been thinking, feeling. He was furious with whoever was doing this to her and angry with himself that he'd left her alone. But overriding all of that was a cold fear that he wasn't doing enough to protect her, wouldn't be able to do enough.

Ruthlessly, he shoved the feelings aside. None of them were helping him.

"Take me over it again," he said, "starting with when woke you up."

As she did, he tried to put himself into the mind of the person who'd taken the time and the opportunity to set up the scene they were both looking at. Whoever it was had been in a position to see what was going on in the library. There were several positions in the woods where an observer might have stationed himself. He might have even chosen to use the garden shed for cover.

"And when I saw the petals," Piper said, "my first reaction was to rush out and give chase. But you'd locked the doors and keyed in the code. That slowed me down enough to think."

Thank God, Duncan thought. If he hadn't slowed her down… He reined his thoughts in.

"If Lightman, Richard and Sid Macks are out, that leaves Cam's library guy or the hoodie guy that Lightman captured on his phone."

"Right." It irked him a bit that she was able to focus more on analyzing the evidence than he was, so he followed her lead. "When I called Daryl, he and Vi were about a half hour away. He'll be able to download what the security cameras captured."

"I'm betting the guy's wearing a hooded sweatshirt, and we won't get a look at his face. He had to be out here waiting and watching. He would have spotted the security cameras."

"Yeah." Duncan reviewed what had led up to the rose petal shower in his mind. "The woods provide plenty of cover. While you were sleeping I opened the doors for a while. I even stepped out to take a call from Cam." He scanned the clearing again. He took his gun out of his backpack and tucked it into the waist of his jeans and continued, "There are lots of places he could have concealed himself. Even in the gardening shed. He could have heard my conversation, then watched me lock up the place and go out to the stones, and he grabbed the opportunity."

"To scare me or to lure me out," Piper said.

"Come with me." He punched the code into the pad, then slid open the doors and drew her with him out to the terrace. Alba followed.

After he re-armed the security, he closed the doors and they moved toward the shed. The door was closed, the padlock secure. Any hope of footprints had been erased by the fury of the storm.

"Whoever was here is long gone," Piper said. "Otherwise Alba would be barking."

Duncan turned to see that the dog hadn't ventured beyond the terrace, and she was digging at something. Pressing a hand to the small of Piper's back, he urged her back to the library doors. Together, they squatted down to see what had caught Alba's attention.

Duncan picked up the small round piece of plastic.

"She found a clue," Piper said.

"Some kind of lens cover. And there's a logo on it, something we can trace. Good girl." He ran a hand over Alba's head, and the dog rubbed against his side.

"She was the one who woke me. And she threw herself against the glass doors. She probably scared the wits out of whoever was out here." When she turned back to Duncan, their knees were nearly brushing. "So you can stop feeling so damn guilty about leaving me alone for a few minutes. You left Alba with me. And I can take care of myself." She used a finger to poke him in the chest and nearly set him toppling back on his heels.

Yes, he thought. She could. And even though she had that Diana-the-Huntress look back in her eyes, he was going to see that she had backup. And to do that, he needed to keep an objective distance. He raised both hands, palms up. "Agreed."

For now.

TWO HOURS LATER, PIPER STOOD in the main parlor of the castle stifling the urge to pace. Once Daryl and Vi had arrived, the men had formed a separate team. While she and Vi had made sandwiches for dinner, they'd worked in Adair's office. Through the open French doors, she watched them still huddled at the computer screen. Duncan stood looking over Daryl's shoulder. He took his reading glasses off, set them aside and pinched the bridge of his nose.

Something pushed at the edge of her mind, but she couldn't quite catch hold of it. Hoping to get another push, she continued to study the two men. They were still running through the pictures from the security cameras. She'd been right about the rose petal person wearing a hooded sweatshirt. The cameras hadn't caught more than pieces of his face. Daryl was using some software program to come up with a composite picture.

What she could clearly read in the body language of the two men was that they weren't having much luck. The lens case Alba had found belonged to a portable telescope with a powerful lens. Not something that could be easily found at a chain store. Daryl had assigned someone in his office to try to trace where it might have been purchased. It proved someone was keeping a close but distant eye on the castle and its grounds.

No big news there.

There hadn't been any useful updates from D.C., either. The only relatively interesting piece of news had been provided by Sheriff Skinner. The vase of roses that had been delivered from Margie's Flowers had been called in from a D.C. florist, and it had been paid for with a stolen credit card over the phone. The call could have been made from anywhere.

She stood there for a few more minutes studying the two men, but whatever was struggling to get foremost into her mind had slipped away again. And she'd found herself just staring at Duncan. He was doing exactly what she'd asked. Keeping his distance. He hadn't touched her since they'd left the stone arch. They were in agreement that they'd chosen the right solution.

So why was she feeling so…restless? Worse, why was she second-guessing herself? Turning on her heel, she went to the kitchen where she knew she'd find her aunt.

The room was filled with the scent of freshly baked cookies, and Vi was pulling a tray out of the oven. The scent and the memories it triggered immediately eased some of her frustration. "Can I help?"

As if in answer, the teakettle began to shrill.

"You can help me load the tea cart. I think the men could use a snack."

"They've formed their own little investigative team," Piper muttered as she made the tea and then loaded cups onto the cart.

"They're worried about you," Vi said.

On the way to the refrigerator, Piper took a cookie off the cooling rack. "I'll be fine. I just…"

"What?"

She turned back to face her aunt, cookie in one hand and a pitcher of cream in the other. "I just want my life to go back to normal. Is that so much to ask?"

Vi took the cream and placed it on the cart. Then she met Piper's eyes. "And what would normal be?"

"My job. My routine. Everything was fine until… dammit." She bit into the cookie, and barely tasted it.

Vi said nothing.

Piper took another bite of cookie, then set it on the counter. "Your cookies used to fix everything," she complained.

Vi stepped forward then and ran a hand down her niece's hair. "What is it you want to fix?"

"I liked my life just fine. It was exactly the way I

wanted it to be. Everything was on track. Until the Lightman case. But I was going to handle that. I still can. But seeing Duncan again has mixed up everything, and I've just made it worse."

Vi took her hands. "How have you made it worse?"

"I just wanted him so much. He wanted me, too. So I came up with a plan that would solve the problem. We're adults, so why shouldn't we have this temporary arrangement? No promises, no strings. It was working. It was great."

"Until...?" Vi prompted.

"I kissed him in the stone arch." There. She'd said it.

Vi squeezed her hands. "And you think he's your true love."

"No." But wasn't that exactly what she was afraid of?

Don't panic.

"He can't be. What we feel for each other is desire." Something that red-hot and primal couldn't be love. "It's chemistry. It'll go away. In the meantime, I told Duncan we have to stop. I mean, it would be dangerous to keep indulging ourselves when there's so much at stake."

Vi nodded. "Yes, the biggest stakes of all. You're afraid of losing your heart. Do you know how Duncan feels?"

"No." Panic surged. "But he agrees with me that we need to step back. Quit while we're ahead."

"He said that to you?"

She lifted her chin. "Actions speak as loudly as words."

Vi placed a hand on Piper's cheek. "Even when you were little, you always had the best arguments. I wish I had a dollar for everything you ever talked me out of."

Piper frowned at her. "What are you saying?"

Vi smiled at her. "That you'll figure this all out. And when you come up with a solution that satisfies you, you'll convince him."

"FRESH BAKED COOKIES," Vi announced as she and Piper entered the main parlor with the tea cart. By the time she had filled the cups, the men had joined them. Daryl sat on the love seat next to Vi. Piper sat on the sofa. And as Duncan pulled out the desk chair and placed it closer to the tea cart, something tightened around her heart. Oh, he'd heard her argument loud and clear. He was keeping his distance, and he looked perfectly happy to do so.

She tried another cookie. Chocolate chip were her favorite, but they tasted like sawdust. She'd made the right decision, she told herself. Break it off before it could get riskier.

And just as soon as they figured out how to put Lightman back in jail and how to stop the crazy person who was sending her flowers, they could both go back to D.C. and make a clean break of it.

"These are spectacular, Vi," Duncan said as he reached for another cookie.

Obviously, they didn't taste like sawdust to him. She picked up her cup of tea and set it right back down.

"I wish we had something more to celebrate," Duncan said. "The good news is one of the security cameras got a couple of partials on the face of the person who tossed rose petals all over the terrace."

"I've sent it to one of my top technicians," Daryl said. "He's working up a full face composite and he'll run it through a facial recognition scanner. However, not everyone is in the system."

"We'll be able to check it against members of the Macks family and the family members of other victims of the RPK," Duncan said. "It will take some time. Which we might not have. Daryl and I were talking about it while we worked."

Daryl waved a hand. "And I agree with Duncan's analysis, so I asked him to fill you in."

Piper's stomach sank. He was totally working with Daryl now. She'd gotten just what she'd asked for. What she'd demanded.

"Until we know for sure, I think we have to assume we're working with three different problems here. Number one, we have Lightman in town—a man motivated by his own self-interests. Then we have the guy in the hoodie who set up the scene in Piper's apartment and keeps sending her vases of roses and threatening notes. And third, we have Cam's library visitor."

"The last two could be the same person," Piper said.

He met her eyes for the first time. "True. But I believe the person who followed us into the caves this morning is interested in the sapphires." He paused to glance up at Eleanor's portrait. "And his determination to have them has become obsessive. Following us into that cave was risky. He may not know for sure yet that we discovered the second sapphire earring, and he could very well see Piper as competition. Or he could believe she found it, and he's furious with her. He may very well have showered those rose petals outside the library today, with the purpose of luring Piper out and eliminating her."

Her stomach didn't sink this time. It froze. "We've already established that I have a very large target on my back. But I'm not leaving the castle. Running away will not solve this."

"His behavior today indicates that he's not only willing to take risks to get what he wants, but that he has an ability to seize the moments that present themselves. That makes him much more dangerous than someone who has to plan everything out in advance."

She met his eyes. "I'm not running."

"Duncan doesn't want you to run," Daryl said. "He wants to cancel the photo shoot tomorrow."

"No." Vi and Piper spoke in unison.

"That's just another kind of running away," Piper argued. "And the castle can't just shut down because I made the mistake of coming here."

Vi rose and joined her on the sofa. "Adair set the shoot up months ago. And we have a wedding scheduled next week. I also have two appointments with prospective clients tomorrow. Plus, Daryl has already vetted the magazine and Russell Arbogast and Deanna Lewis."

"I have some men digging deeper on both of them as we speak," Daryl said.

"There'll be strangers on the grounds," Duncan said, speaking directly to Piper. "This person almost lured you out of the castle when there were just the two of us here. There'll be more opportunities tomorrow." He shifted his gaze to Vi. "And the shut-down wouldn't be permanent. We just need more time to gather information."

Piper gripped Vi's hand in hers. "We've got top-notch agents from the FBI and the CIA here in the house and Sheriff Skinner plans to be present for the photo shoot. Aunt Vi and I are smart. We won't do anything stupid. And we have Alba."

Daryl gave Duncan an I-told-you-so look. "Then we'll have to go with Plan B."

"Not until you run it by us," Vi said.

"No negotiations on this one," Daryl said in a flat, no-nonsense tone. "If we're going forward on schedule tomorrow, Piper is confined to working in the library all day, and she's going to wear a wire just in case somebody gets past the security."

"Fine," Piper said. "I'll wear a wire and work on the Lightman files."

Duncan looked as if he was going to say something. But he didn't. Something tightened around her heart.

"You ladies should get some sleep," Daryl said. "Duncan and I will clear the tea cart. Then we'll work a little longer, but tomorrow is going to be a long day."

She'd won her case, Piper thought as Duncan followed Daryl out of the room. She wasn't running away. But it was the argument she'd made earlier when they'd been in the stone arch that was bothering her. Once this was over, she'd make another case to Duncan. Because she wasn't going to let him run away, either.

13

DUNCAN KNEW THAT HE WASN'T going to sleep. He didn't have to waste time lying in his bed and staring at the ceiling to figure that out. So at midnight, instead of following Daryl up the wide staircase to the second floor, he'd slipped out of the castle to walk on the castle grounds. The storm that had thundered through earlier had left a clear sky peppered with stars. With the moonlight, there was plenty of light to see by as he made his way through the gardens.

He rarely experienced restlessness or felt at loose ends, but those were exactly the feelings that had been plaguing him since he'd seen those rose petals strewn outside the library. He could deal with the cold hard fear that had settled like one of Angus One's stones in his stomach. But the other two were more problematic. Because they'd been triggered by Piper.

He could have holed himself up in the library and distracted himself with the Lightman files, but that wouldn't have brought him any closer to solving his problem. When he reached the stone arch, he stepped into it and then turned. What he saw first was the gardens, then the castle and the gleam of the lake below, all surrounded by the darkness of the mountains and the trees.

Angus One could have built the stone arch anywhere on the estate, so he must have taken care with the selection of this spot. He also must have stood here many times, with Eleanor's hand in his, looking at what they'd created together. And they'd risked everything to do it.

Over the years, he'd never given much thought to the legend of the stone arch. Why would he? At ten, he'd been much more fascinated by the missing sapphires. Even when he'd stood here and heard his mother make her vows to A.D., it hadn't been the legend he'd thought of. Once he'd looked into Piper's eyes, he hadn't been able to think much at all.

That's what had scared him off. He was a rational man and she had the power to make him lose his control over that. In fact, he'd never been able to rationalize what he felt for her. Not then. Certainly, not now. He wanted her, needed her to a point way beyond reason.

Was that love? And what did she feel for him?

Those were the questions that had sent him into default mode. When she'd demanded that they break everything off, he'd agreed because he understood her decision. He hadn't lied to her or to the others when he'd said that the person who'd strewn those petals on the terrace was unpredictable, and therefore dangerous. Perhaps even more dangerous than Patrick Lightman. The RPK was a creature of habit, pattern, bound by ritual. The person who had followed them into the cave that morning wasn't. Duncan needed to put Piper's safety first.

And by going along with her, he'd slipped comfortably back into his own pattern—being cautious and staying on the sidelines. Nothing of what he was seeing right now would have been here if Angus One and Eleanor had been either cautious or predictable.

To hell with rationality, he decided as he stepped out of the arch and strode toward the castle.

When he reached her room, Duncan slipped in quietly and closed the door behind him. Moonlight poured through the closed balcony doors. The tangled sheets spoke of restlessness, of a battle hard fought and won. So like his Piper. Now she lay curled into a ball with one arm tucked beneath a pillow, her breathing even.

He recalled watching her sleep before and wanting her mindlessly. That hadn't changed. What had changed was the very different rush of emotion he experienced now. For a moment he saw what it might be like to see her like this every night and every morning, and something inside of him opened.

Moving soundlessly, he slipped out of his shoes and clothes before he joined her on the bed. When he drew her close, she pressed herself against him and settled. He kissed her first on the cheek and then very softly on her mouth. Her lips were warm and softened by sleep. Her taste was almost familiar now. He let himself absorb the sensations, drift with them.

He heard the moment she awakened, a sound of pleasure, a quick gasp of surprise. Her nails dug into his shoulder as she drew back and opened her eyes.

"Duncan. We said… We agreed." But she didn't push him away, and her body remained soft against his.

"I can't sleep for wanting you, Piper." He whispered the words against her lips. "Let me touch you. Show you how much. Just for tonight."

She didn't have the strength to say no. How could

she form the word when his mouth was nibbling at hers? And she'd been dreaming of this, wanting him to come to her, yearning for the pleasure of his mouth, his hands on her.

But this wasn't a dream. His heart beat fast and steady beneath her palm, and the pulse of it echoed her own. She wanted to touch him, to offer him as much pleasure as he was giving her. So she did, testing the strength of his shoulders, feeling those smooth muscles flex beneath her hands.

There was no need to hurry or rush. Time was a gift they offered each other as they lay loving each other in the moonlight. Steeped in him, she whispered requests and murmured in pleasure when he granted them. Should she have known how tenderness both given and received could make her aware of every pore and pulse of her body?

Even when he moved over her and made a place for himself between her legs, there was none of the speed and the fury that they'd brought each other before. She absorbed every detail of him, the gleam of those dark eyes, the strong lines of that warrior face. Framing it with her hands, she drew it closer until their lips melded, parted and then touched again. She would remember seeing him this way forever. Her throat ached when he linked his fingers with hers and pressed their joined hands into the tangle of sheets.

She spoke only his name as he slipped into her and filled her completely. The sound aroused him unbearably, but he kept the pace slow and easy. With their minds and needs fused, she moved with him and gave everything.

As desire built, her taste darkened, her body shuddered for more. So he gave her more. As he felt her crest, he clung to control and guided her up and over the next climax. And the next.

And when he knew she thought only of him, he finally gave his own needs their freedom and poured himself into her.

DUNCAN STOOD JUST OUTSIDE THE main foyer of the castle, in the hallway that ran back to the library and the kitchen. From his position, he could make sure that no one wandered back to the library area and still keep everyone in view. Deanna Lewis was halfway up the stairs taking shots of the stained-glass windows on the landing. She'd impressed him yesterday as competent and efficient. She carried a notebook with her and consulted it frequently, especially when she gave instructions to the two young assistants she'd brought along.

The trio had started with the main parlor and moved on to the formal dining room and the ballroom that was used for many of the wedding receptions. Currently, the two young men were outside the main entrance taking a break. Through the glass panels, he could see that Sheriff Skinner had engaged them in conversation.

Across the hall, he could see Daryl and Vi in the main parlor where Richard Arbogast was having tea. The senior editor had been disappointed when he'd learned that Piper wouldn't be available for an interview. When he'd once again tried to convince Vi to let his photographer take a few shots of the library, Duncan had almost intervened. But Vi had diverted Arbogast's attention by including him in a tour she was giving to a prospective bride and groom. They'd been fascinated with his knowledge of Scottish castles, and now Vi was rewarding him with homemade scones and stories about her girls growing up in a castle. He could see why she and Adair were building such a successful business.

So far everything was quiet. In D.C., Glen Loch and here at the castle. Daryl's tech man hadn't gotten back to him with any news about the composite photo yet. Patrick Lightman had appeared at the diner for a late breakfast, and then sat on a bench to take in the view of the lake, just as he had the day before. Currently, he was back in his room at the Eagle's Nest taking a nap. His snores were being recorded by Skinner's deputy.

Duncan couldn't have asked for a less eventful morning. But waiting on the sidelines for something to happen had never frustrated him so much. He could only hope that Piper was having more luck with the RPK files. Daryl had fitted her with a wire that was voice activated. Both he and Daryl wore a small earpiece, but so far Piper hadn't made a sound. Vi and Daryl had each checked in with her, but the news had been the same. Nothing.

He glanced back over his shoulder at the closed library door. She'd be safe enough there until everyone left.

"Mr. Sutherland?"

Duncan turned his attention to Deanna Lewis as she came down the main staircase. She was an attractive woman in her late twenties and she was dressed in the same comfortable jeans and T-shirt she'd worn the day before. "You could do me a big favor."

"And that would be?"

"There's a library here." She raised a hand. "I know Russell was told that it's closed to the public and not really ready to be photographed. But this is my first freelance assignment with a magazine of *Architectural Digest*'s prestige. If there's any way you could make an exception and let me take a few shots, it would really earn me points with my boss."

"I'm sorry, but the library is off-limits. After the death of the current owner's wife, it was locked up and unused for years," Duncan said. "I can't see why you'd want a shot of it."

"Because it's off-limits," she said. "Forbidden. I don't always want to be taking pictures for a magazine—I'm more interested in photojournalism."

Russell Arbogast entered the foyer. "Deanna, I'm going to pay a last visit to the stone arch with Daryl and Vi. Do you need any more shots of it?"

"I've got what I need, but why don't you take Sam and Carl? It will be good practice for them."

As soon as everyone left, Deanna turned back to Duncan. "How about letting me take a few shots of the library from the outside? I took some pictures of the grounds yesterday, but I'm not even sure where the library is located."

Duncan studied her. Her curiosity seemed genuine. But it also occurred to him that if she'd been taking outside shots yesterday, she might quite easily have found the library on her own. It wouldn't be hard to spot a library through the glass doors. If you used the telescopic lens on the camera, you could easily identify it from quite a distance away in the woods.

His own curiosity aroused, Duncan said, "I'll show you where it's located, but no shots through the windows."

She beamed a smile at him. "Deal."

PIPER CLOSED THE LID ON BOX number five of the RPK files and stretched her arms over her head. A glance at her watch told her that she'd been working on it for more than two hours. Nothing had popped.

Standing, she walked to the sliding glass doors that led to the terrace and swept her gaze around the clearing. She'd decided to work at the desk so that she could keep an eye out in case someone decided to throw rose petals all over the terrace again.

So far, no one had.

There was something, some detail that she was missing. Something important. Her first inkling had been at the diner yesterday when she'd been sitting across from Lightman. And twice later in the day she'd experienced that little mental nudge, but she couldn't latch onto it.

She needed to talk to Duncan. If he could just take her through the conversation they'd had with Lightman in that methodical way he had, she might remember.

Or she might just be making up an excuse to see Duncan again. He'd left her room before she'd awakened.

And that had hurt. She rubbed the heel of her hand against her chest where it still did.

Just for tonight.

That's what he'd said to her. He'd never promised her any more. In the beginning, even in the stone arch yesterday, she hadn't wanted any more.

She certainly hadn't wanted to fall in love with him. But that's just what she'd done. She rubbed her hand again over the ache in her chest. Now she would pay the price—the same price her father had paid for loving her mother. Loss.

She wasn't even aware that her vision had blurred with tears until she saw Duncan walk into the clearing outside the glass. Blinking, she recognized his companion as the photographer who'd been with Russell Arbogast the day before. Deanna Lewis. For one second, she was tempted to punch in the security code and step out to say hello. But they weren't walking toward her. Then she remembered, Russell had asked to take photos of the library, and Vi had told them it wouldn't be available. So what were they doing here?

Her mind had barely considered the question when Deanna set her camera down and pulled out her notebook. Duncan took it and put on his reading glasses to study it.

That's when the memory struck her like a bare-fisted punch.

Reading glasses.

Images flashed into her mind at fast-forward speed. The first pair she'd seen on him had been right here in the library. She recalled him setting them aside on the desk and also handing them to him in the stone arch. If she hadn't found them on the ledge, he might have left them behind.

Patrick Lightman had said he didn't need the glasses he'd worn during the trial all the time. But he'd pulled them out yesterday when he'd been looking at the video clip on his cell phone and replaced them later in his pocket.

The memory tugged hard this time. There was something she'd seen in one of the files.

Which one? Whirling away from the glass doors, she strode back to the boxes neatly lined up along the wall and squatted down in front of them. She'd been working on the fourth box yesterday when she'd fallen asleep. Crime scene photos of one of the RPK killer's earlier victims.

Piper sat down on the floor, located the file, and

removed the photos. Then she spread them out, examining each shot before she placed it on the floor. The RPK had staged his scenes so exactly and the details were so similar that it was hard to distinguish one from another.

But something in this particular one had stuck with her. The body lying in the center of the sheet had been shot from different angles, and a zoom lens had effectively captured close-ups of different sections of the scene.

She spotted it in the third photo—a pair of glasses lying just beneath the couch. They rested on the top of the lens frame with the temple wings spread out—just as if someone had set them down for a minute. Yesterday, Duncan had set his on the desk in the same way when she'd ordered him to take them off. And she could see it—just the shadow of a logo on the side. It was the same one she'd seen on the glasses Lightman had used in the diner and on the ones he'd worn during the trial.

In her mind, she tried to picture it the way Duncan would. Lightman working, totally focused on setting up his victim and getting the scene perfect. He slips off his glasses and sets them down and in adjusting the sheet they somehow slip beneath the edge of the couch. Or perhaps he slides them away to allow for a perfect fall of rose petals.

And then, in his focus on the crime, he forgets and leaves them behind.

Those glasses had to be in an evidence bag somewhere. Someone had probably assumed they belonged to the victim. They'd probably never been tested for prints. Or if they had, Lightman hadn't been a suspect then. Daryl could probably enlarge the photo and get a clearer image of that telling logo. There was a very good chance that Patrick Lightman could now be connected to at least one of the RPK's other victims.

She glanced at the other boxes. Maybe Lightman had left things behind more than once. Excitement had her surging to her feet. She had to tell Duncan. Thank heavens he was still in the clearing. Punching in the code, she disarmed the alarm and then raced onto the terrace.

"Piper, no. Go back."

The shouted words had her freezing in her tracks. But only for a second. When she saw him crumple to the ground, she raced forward. There was a buzzing in her head as she dropped to her knees. "Duncan."

He didn't answer, and he was lying so still.

"What happened?" But when she glanced up at Deanna Lewis and saw the gun, she knew. "You shot him."

"Not yet," she said in a pleasant tone. "Too much noise. I used a very high-powered Taser. And I have to thank you for coming out. You distracted him just enough. I was having a problem convincing him to let me come into the library."

Duncan wasn't dead. That thought helped clear her mind, and she remembered she was wired. Daryl would have heard everything once she started speaking. He'd be on his way right now. She just had to stall.

Piper forced her gaze away from Duncan and away from the gun to meet the young woman's eyes. The hate she saw there nearly had her taking a quick step back. "Why are you doing this?"

"Why? Because Eleanor Campbell MacPherson's sapphires don't belong to you. And you can't find them before I do. So you have to be eliminated."

Eliminated? For the first time the realization hit

her that the woman she was looking at wasn't entirely sane. *Obsessed*—that was the word Duncan had used. "You're the person who was visiting the library, aren't—?"

Piper broke off when she saw Deanna shift the barrel of the gun toward Duncan's head.

"Stop talking. I'll use the gun on him first and then on you unless you agree to come with me now. Your choice."

No time to wait for Daryl. "Don't shoot Duncan." Piper rose to her feet. "Spare his life and I'll take you to the sapphires. They're what you want, aren't they? They're why you visited the library, trying to find some clue to their location?"

"They belong to us. They always did. And now it's our mission to find them. Not yours."

"I'll do more than go with you. I'll show you where they are. Duncan and I found a second sapphire earring in the caves. I can take you there."

Deanna hesitated for just a moment. "I followed you and I looked. If it was there, you took it away."

"We heard you following us, so we hid it well. To protect it." It was such a huge lie that she wondered how her nose didn't grow like Pinocchio's. And Piper was pretty sure it wouldn't stand up to logical scrutiny. Why on earth, if they'd found the sapphire earring, would they have left it behind? But Duncan's theory was that the woman she was looking at right now was obsessed with getting hold of Eleanor's dowry. And she was just as obsessed with getting her away from Duncan. "I can show you exactly where. The necklace may be there, too. We didn't have time to search for it."

"All right."

Piper didn't even allow herself a breath of relief before she turned and headed toward the cliff face.

TOO MUCH PAIN, DUNCAN THOUGHT. It swam in his head and streaked through his muscles with an intensity that nearly blocked out the fear. He couldn't move. He could barely think. *Piper.* Each second that ticked by, Deanna Lewis was getting her farther and farther away from the castle. Eyes closed, Duncan put all his effort into getting control over his body.

He opened his eyes first, blinking against the blinding sun. But he knew that he was recovering when the fear began to push out the pain. The second time he opened his eyes, he was able to raise his hand to shade them. And he knew a brief flash of relief when he saw Daryl, Vi and Sheriff Skinner rush out through the sliding terrace doors from the library.

He'd managed to sit up by the time they reached him.

"Deanna Lewis," he managed.

Daryl squatted down beside him. "Don't try to talk. Piper let us know they're headed to the caves."

"Caves," Duncan repeated.

"Piper told Deanna that you and she had left the earring hidden there. She even suggested that the necklace might be there also."

Brilliant, Duncan thought. But when Deanna found out it was a lie, the strategy could prove lethal for Piper.

"You think she's the person you saw running away wearing the hoodie," Sheriff Skinner said.

Duncan managed to nod and didn't like the way his head swam.

"When Piper asked her, she didn't deny being the

person who paid all those patient visits to the library," Daryl said.

"She's not patient anymore," Duncan said. "Arbogast?"

"I got a man babysitting him and the two young photographers at the stones. They're not going anywhere, and my deputy is on his way out here. He called me a few minutes ago to tell me that Lightman isn't in his room. Seems the snoring that's been going on for the last couple of hours has come from a mini tape recorder Lightman set up."

"I'll follow along the cliff path," Daryl said, rising.

Duncan grabbed Cam's boss by the ankle. "She won't hesitate to kill Piper. If the profile I've been building is right, there's a good chance she blames Piper because she didn't find the jewels first. The kinds of risks she's running—like revealing herself today—mean she's very dangerous. She may not even be worried about being caught."

He could talk again, breathe. He made his way unsteadily to his feet.

"What's the plan?" Daryl asked.

"We're going to the cave through an alternate route. You got a flashlight?"

Daryl patted his pocket. "Always. Along with my gun."

Duncan fished in his pocket for his own. "This way." He could only pray that he and Daryl would make it in time.

14

Don't panic. Piper repeated the phrase in her head, keeping the pace fast as the path wound upward to the cliffs. The sun was behind them, casting long shadows in front of them, so she knew just where Deanna was without looking back. She'd given some thought to running. But as fast as she was, a bullet was faster. And if she did outrun it, crazy Deanna might decide to go back and shoot Duncan while he lay helpless on the ground.

Talk. That was her safest alternative, Piper decided. It might save both of them from panicking. At the very least, it would keep Deanna from wondering why she and Duncan had decided to leave a priceless earring in the caves.

"Why were you visiting the library?" Piper asked.

"Because there had to be something there. Some clue to the whereabouts of the Stuart Sapphires. Anyone could have figured that out once the *Times* ran that picture of Mary Stuart wearing them side-by-side with Eleanor Campbell MacPherson's wedding portrait. And there hasn't been a trace of them since Eleanor died. They have to be here. We just needed more time. Your sister found the first one and cut off our access to the library."

"You're sure that Eleanor's dowry and the jewels Mary Stuart wore at her coronation are the same?"

"I'm sure. We've seen the original of the picture the *Times* ran, and we've seen the portrait of Eleanor. And the Stuart Sapphires were never Eleanor's dowry. They were a gift to our family. And she stole them. Just as you're trying to steal them now."

They weren't Eleanor's dowry? Could that be true? Or was crazy Deanna just spinning a fantasy? Piper had to hope that Daryl was getting everything down. They'd reached the part of the path that cut deeper into the woods. The light around them dimmed and the scent of pine filled the air. Out of the corner of her eye, she thought she saw a flash of movement about fifteen feet to her left. Not Duncan. He couldn't possibly have gotten here this quickly. Daryl?

Whoever it was, she had to keep Deanna's attention totally focused on her. So she stumbled and fell.

The sound of the gun discharging was so loud it made her ears ring, and she felt the heat of the passing bullet on the skin of her arm.

"Get up," Deanna said. "And don't try that again."

"I won't." But Piper took as much time as she dared shoving herself to her feet while she scanned the areas in her peripheral vision. To her left, and much closer to the edge of the woods and the cliff face, she saw exactly what she was hoping for—another shadow moving from tree to tree. She purposely led the way on a slant to the right, saying, "The cliff face isn't far, and the caves should be right where we come out through the trees."

Then she prayed that Daryl would have time to get there first.

DUNCAN FELT HIS HEART STOP WHEN the sound of a bullet exploded in his earpiece. If he hadn't just dropped into the small cave behind Tinker's Falls, he might have raced into the woods. As it was, the instant Daryl dropped beside him, he moved to grab the edge of the opening, intending to climb out again.

Daryl grabbed his arm. "She's okay."

Through the ringing in his ears, Duncan made out the voices again.

"If you try to trick me again…if you try anything, I won't miss the next time. I wanted you to come up here so that I could eliminate you. And I will if you don't take me to the sapphires."

"I'm not going to trick you, Deanna. We're only about a hundred feet away from the cliff face, and I'm going to show you where the sapphires are."

Duncan let out a breath. She was not only okay, she was letting them know exactly where they were and she was refocusing Deanna's attention on what she was after.

"You okay?" Daryl asked.

"Yes." If Piper could keep her head, so would he. She'd lead Deanna to the third cave, the one where she'd found the earring. In his mind, he pictured their climb down the cliff face and the route they would have to follow to get to the third cave. He and Daryl had a shorter distance to cover, but the narrow tunnel would slow them down.

Quickly, he gave Daryl an overview of the terrain. "Watch your head," he warned as he dropped to his knees and led the way into the first tunnel.

"YOU CLIMB DOWN FIRST," Deanna said. "When you get to the cave, step to the side of the ledge, but keep in sight. I won't hesitate to shoot."

She might not have to waste a bullet, Piper thought as she looked down and gauged the distance to the ledge.

"Now," Deanna urged.

Piper took as much time as she dared sitting down on the edge of the cliff and dropping her legs over. There'd been no sign of the figure she'd seen in the woods. Daryl, she was hoping. Maybe he'd had time to climb down to the cave.

Best-case scenario, he was waiting inside right now, and all she had to do was get to the ledge. In her mind, she tried to remember the instructions Duncan had called up to her. Was it only yesterday? Turning onto her stomach, she searched for and found her first toe-hold.

Think. If Daryl wasn't there, she was good at finding solutions. She'd figure a way out of this. She searched for and found another place to set her foot. First she had to get down to the cave. Pushing fear and everything else aside, she focused her full attention on the climb. One minute, two minutes went by. Every muscle was straining, and she could feel sweat dripping down her back, but she reached the point where the stones had cascaded down on her.

There wasn't far to go. If she could just reach the ledge, she knew the caves and tunnels. She might be able to get away. Deanna had followed Duncan and her to the third cave, but Piper knew the way out. Deanna didn't. Clinging to the rocks, she twisted her head and made herself look down. Too far. She couldn't drop yet. She had to get closer.

Glancing up, she saw Deanna start down. The woman was both agile and fast, and Piper didn't dare rush. When she was finally within jumping distance of the ledge, she glanced up again and saw that Deanna was only a few feet above her, braced against the cliff face with her gun out.

"Drop to the ledge, but stay where I can see you," Deanna said.

Holding her breath, Piper let go of her death grip on the rock she was holding and dropped. She had time to glance into the cave, and her heart leaped. She'd been right. Someone was indeed standing in the darkness just inside.

When Deanna landed lightly on the balls of her feet, her gun hand steady, the shadowy stranger moved quickly, striking Deanna on the head. She fell like a rock, her camera smashing on the rocks, her gun sliding over the ledge and clattering down the cliff face. Then Piper found herself looking into Patrick Lightman's blue eyes.

Her mind began to race nearly as fast as her heart. Details registered in flashes. The gun in his hand, blood oozing from Deanna's head and staining the stones. She had questions—so many that her head ached with them. And Lightman could answer some of them. "Patrick, what are you doing here?"

"I followed you and Ms. Lewis, of course."

"Why?" The biggest question at the back of her mind was if Patrick Lightman was the shadow she'd seen in the woods, where were Daryl and Duncan?

Had Duncan been injured more seriously than she'd thought? Wasn't the wire she was wearing working?

"I told you in the diner yesterday that you were in danger," Patrick said in a calm voice. "She didn't wish you well. She'd been studying your movements in D.C. for a while."

"She was the person you filmed wearing the hooded sweatshirt. The one who set up that scene in my apartment?"

"Yes. I actually admired her style until she did that amateurish job, but then I knew I had to put a stop to it."

"Why didn't you tell us all that yesterday? Why did you throw suspicion on Sid Macks?"

"Because I hadn't decided what to do about Ms. Lewis yet." Then he smiled at her, and the glee in his eyes had the panic inside of her threatening to break free again. "After all, she does fit my profile."

Keep calm. Keep him talking. And think. "I don't understand. Why would you have to do anything about her?"

His smile faded abruptly and some of the calmness faded from his voice. "Because she had decided to stalk you, and you belong to me. The ones who came before you—they were nothing. All they did was to bring me to you. You've been mine ever since you set me free. No one else can have you."

Piper recognized what she was seeing in his eyes. Not merely madness, but obsession. And she remembered what Duncan had said. True obsession destroyed rationality.

But Duncan would be thinking in a rational way. He couldn't think any other way. The certainty of that helped her focus. She'd made sure to say quite clearly where she and Deanna were going. And Duncan would never have followed her along the cliff path. He would be with Daryl even now entering the caves from the other entrance at Tinker's Falls. And he'd be expecting her to lead Deanna into that third cave where they'd found the earring.

Now she wouldn't be leading Deanna anywhere. So she had to keep Patrick Lightman talking.

"Do you know why Deanna was following me in D.C.?"

"Not at first." He glanced down at the very still body of Deanna Lewis. "I checked into her background and learned that she was a photographer. So I thought she wanted to hurt me by stirring up all those nasty stories in the press again. But after she staged that scene in your apartment, I knew she wanted to hurt you. And I was right."

"You followed her up here."

"I followed you both up here. I protect what's mine. I overheard her talking on her cell phone this morning and telling someone that she intended to make her move today to eliminate you. She suspected that you'd found the second earring and that you were searching the library for the location of the necklace. It made her furious. She knew that you were being protected by the FBI and the CIA and she was still going to find a way to hurt you. So I did what I had to do."

"Do you know who she was talking to?" Piper asked. "Did she say why she wanted to eliminate me?"

Lightman shrugged. "The sapphires. She believes they belong to her. Just as I believe you belong to me." He raised the gun and pointed it at her. "I'm a little more wary of the FBI and the CIA than she was. I'm sure they'll be along shortly, so we'll climb down together. Ready?"

READY WAS THE LAST THING HE was, Duncan thought as he and Daryl finally reached the cave where he and Piper had found the earring. He'd kept the fear and anger on a very tight leash as he'd listened to that maniac talk about his obsession with her. Instead, he'd focused his energy on crawling as fast as he could through the narrow tunnel near the falls. But the thought of her having to climb down to the beach with Lightman had his fear threatening to take control.

All he could think was that he hadn't said nearly enough to her last night and he'd kept his distance all day. He hadn't told her what she'd come to mean to him. He hadn't told her he loved her. So they had to get to her in time. And they still had two tunnels and a cave to go.

Crossing the cave where they'd found the earring, he'd stepped into the next tunnel with Daryl close behind when he heard Piper's voice again. "They're going to know I'm missing by now. Sheriff Skinner will be looking all along the lake for Deanna and me."

"We'll have to take our chances," Lightman said.

"My sisters and I played a lot in these caves when we were little," Piper said. "I know another way out."

Duncan met Daryl's eyes as silence stretched for three beats.

"Tell me about this other way out," Lightman finally said.

"This is the first of three caves connected by tunnels that finally reach to ground level. We'll come out in the woods near a waterfall."

Two more beats of silence.

"I'll hold the flashlight," Lightman said. "Lead the way."

"She's bringing him to us," Duncan whispered to Daryl. "We have to beat them to the center cave."

Piper spoke over him. "The tunnel to the first cave is short. And there's this big boulder in the middle cave that we'll have to get around. It'll take some time. And the second tunnel is longer."

Duncan immediately held a hand up to Daryl. She was talking as much to him as to Lightman, reminding him of the layout. Signaling him? She was right about the fact that the first tunnel was the shortest. He spoke softly again to Daryl. "I think she has a plan. We'll get as close as we can to the end of this tunnel and still keep out of sight." Then he pulled out his gun. Daryl did the same.

PIPER FORCED HERSELF TO breathe in and out slowly, evenly, as she led the way to the center cave. She could only hope that Duncan had read between the lines of what she'd been saying to Lightman. More, she hoped her plan would work. To give it just a little more credibility, she slid on some of the loose stones underfoot and slapped her hand against the side wall of the tunnel. "Watch your step," she said to Lightman.

"Watch yours," he said back to her.

The fact that he was holding the flashlight and her body blocked much of the light slowed their progress. If he'd given it to her, she might have used it as a weapon. But Lightman was no dummy. So she was going to have to use what came to hand. When they stepped into the center cave, he swept the light around, throwing long shadows on the walls before he let it come to rest on the opening of the next tunnel.

There was enough spillage for her to get a good look at the large boulder that had once blocked off most of the tunnel. There were plenty of pebbles and rocks at its base. Without giving herself the chance to think any further, she strode toward it. The instant her foot struck some of the stones, she let it slide out from beneath her, then fell, making sure to hit her head as hard as she dared against the boulder on the way down. She heard the sound of the impact, saw stars, and fell so that she landed on her side. Before he could get the light fully aimed at her, she wrapped her fingers tightly around a rock the size of a baseball.

"Get up. You tried that same trick to distract Ms. Lewis. It won't work with me."

"Hit…my…head." The beam of light blinded her, but it pinpointed his position. It also allowed her to see the gleaming chrome of the gun. She sat up, careful to keep the rock out of his sight.

"Get up," he repeated.

He wasn't going to come any closer. By the time she threw the rock, he'd have a bullet in her. Then she heard exactly what she'd been hoping for, a slide of rocks in the tunnel behind her.

Lightman shifted his gun and the light toward the tunnel's opening. Piper used all her strength to hurl the rock at him. She heard the sound of it hitting flesh and bone before two shots rang out nearly simultaneously. She saw Lightman pitch to the ground and heard the crash of his flashlight. Then for a moment everything went black.

"Stay down." It was Duncan's voice.

She was perfectly happy to obey the order. Her head ached. Every bone in her body ached.

"I'll take care of Lightman." Daryl's voice now. She saw two shadows rush out of the tunnel. "You see to Piper."

Aiming his flashlight at her, Duncan dropped to his knees. "You're bleeding. Did he shoot you?"

"I'm fine." She touched her forehead gingerly and felt the blood. "I did that to myself. I had to make it look good when I fell."

She had, Duncan thought. Too good. He'd heard her head connect with that boulder. He used the flashlight to check her eyes, but the pupils weren't dilated.

"Lightman isn't shot, either," Daryl said. "Looks like she knocked him out cold with a rock."

The relief that rushed through Duncan erupted in a laugh as he sat down beside her and scooped her onto his lap. "I don't know why I was worried about you." Then he lowered his mouth to hers and, trembling, he found everything. Everything.

"If you two want to come up for air for a minute," Daryl said, "I've got some more good news."

"What?" Duncan raised his head, but he didn't loosen his hold on Piper.

"Lightman has some interesting items in his backpack—a white sheet, several plastic bags filled with rose petals. I'd say this stuff, along with what I recorded from the wire on Piper, should be enough to send him away for a very long time."

"Are his reading glasses in there?" Piper asked.

"They are," Daryl said.

"They're going to connect him to at least one other RPK victim." Then she told them what she'd discovered in the file. "They have to be in an evidence bag somewhere, and they may have his prints on them. I'll bet he doesn't even remember he left them behind. And you may even be able to trace his purchases. Those are expensive designer frames."

Daryl glanced over at her. "You sure you want to practice law? I could use someone with your eye for detail in my office."

"The FBI could use her, too," Duncan said.

"I can't get a signal on my cell," Daryl said. "How far is it to the outside of this place?"

"Fifteen feet or so through that tunnel," Duncan said.

"I'll let Sheriff Skinner and Vi know that we're all safe and sound, and I'll check on Ms. Lewis."

For a few minutes after he was gone, Piper stayed right where she was with her head pressed into Duncan's shoulder. Just a few more minutes, she told herself. She'd be fine in just a few more minutes.

"It's my fault," Duncan said. "I convinced you to come up here. And I brought her around to the library."

She raised her head and looked him straight in the eye. "Enough. Stop that right now. I agreed to come up here, and I'm the one who broke the rules by rushing out to tell you about my discovery in the files. There's enough blame to go around. And I'm really, really tired of dealing with irrational people today. Those two were total fruitcakes. What I need more than anything else is for you to kiss me again."

When he tightened his arms around her and lowered his mouth to hers, she poured herself into the kiss. He was here holding her, and she felt her fears drain. She'd needed this. And she needed more. So much more. She wanted...

Daryl cleared his throat when he reentered the cave.

When Duncan broke off the kiss, he said, "I've got Deanna Lewis secured. She took quite a blow on the head. Skinner's notifying the trauma center in Albany. He's already called in the state police. They're on their way to the cliff face right now."

Duncan helped Piper get to her feet. "I have to call my boss. She'll probably want someone from the FBI office in Albany to take Lightman into custody. Can you make it out to the ledge?"

"Sure." Every bone in her body ached when she got to her feet. The adrenaline rush was over. But Patrick Lightman was trussed up like a turkey, and she and the people she loved were fine.

15

THE LATE-AFTERNOON SUN SLANTED long shadows over the patio at the back of the kitchen as Duncan put steaks on the grill. He felt as though the day was never going to end. He'd wanted to talk to Piper alone, but one thing after another had interfered, the latest being a celebration dinner that Vi had insisted on. Sheriff Skinner had been invited to stay, and then the men had been assigned to grill duty while the women made salad.

Daryl stepped out of the kitchen with three beers. "The ladies are chilling champagne, but I told Vi we'd start off with these."

Sheriff Skinner took one of the offered bottles. "I propose a toast to a job well done."

Duncan took one of the bottles and raised it. "It's not over yet." His eyes strayed to Piper inside the kitchen. She was tearing lettuce into a bowl. And for a moment he felt the same thing he'd felt when he'd slipped uninvited into her bedroom last night—just an inkling of what it might be like to see her do that ordinary task again and again.

"You're referring to the fact that Deanna Lewis wasn't working alone," Skinner said.

"We listened to her say 'we' and 'us' several times while we were crawling through those tunnels," Daryl said. "And Lightman overhead her making a phone call to someone telling them that she planned to eliminate Piper."

"I think Russell Arbogast is in the clear," Skinner said. "His credentials seem genuine, and he claims he knew nothing about Deanna Lewis's reasons for taking on the job of photographing the castle. But he says she was the one who pitched the idea to him, and the portfolio she showed him of her freelance work was impressive. Her résumé checked out."

"When Arbogast first approached Adair and Vi, I ran a thorough background check on him," Daryl said. "I should have dug deeper on Deanna Lewis, but my impression was the same as Arbogast's. There was nothing there to raise any alarm. I have someone working on her now."

A hissing noise from the grill made Duncan glance back at his steaks. "Whoever Deanna was referring to and talking to on her cell has to be connected to both her and the sapphires. She told Piper that they were given to *their* family, and that Eleanor stole them. I've called Cam. He and Adair, along with A.D. and my mother, have been visiting the Campbell estate. It may be that Deanna Lewis is a descendent of the Campbell family, or she may believe she is. The story that's been passed down is that Angus stole his bride."

"So, some descendent of the Campbell family might believe that she had no right to the dowry and therefore stole them?" Skinner asked.

"That's one theory." Duncan sipped his beer. "Cam's

going to see what he can find out. Deanna also claimed that the sapphires weren't Eleanor's dowry. If not, how did she come into possession of them? My mom is already trying to trace how the jewels made their way from Mary Stuart's coronation to Eleanor Campbell MacPherson."

"In the meantime, the state police are tracing the calls on Lewis's phone, and the trauma center will let you know the moment she regains consciousness," Skinner said. "The bad news is that due to the severity of her injury, that may not happen anytime soon. She's slipped into a coma."

Which meant that Deanna was a temporary dead end when it came to information. Duncan flipped the steaks. "There's still someone out there who is after Eleanor's dowry."

"Any ideas about him or her?" Skinner asked. "You're the profiler."

"I'm thinking, I'm hoping, that Deanna's partner is more rational," Duncan said. "Whoever decided that Eleanor must have hidden the sapphires had the same basic idea that I did. The plan to search the library for some clue to the location of the jewels is exactly where I might have begun. And he was patient. Deanna wasn't. But until we track that person down, we can't be sure any of the MacPherson women are safe."

"They're going to be as safe as we can make them. And we may have answers soon." Daryl put a hand on Duncan's shoulder. "In the meantime you and Piper have taken a dangerous serial killer off the street, you've captured one of the persons who was sneaking into the library, and you've found the second of Eleanor's earrings. Any one of those things is worth a good steak any day. Even if we have to eventually wash it down with champagne."

"I can drink to that," Skinner said. The three men raised their bottles in a toast.

PIPER THOUGHT THE MEAL WOULD never end. Not that she didn't enjoy the steak and the champagne. It was just that since they'd come back from the cave, she hadn't had a moment to think or to plan. Or to talk to Duncan.

There'd been so many people, asking so many questions—first the state police, then the FBI. Her cell phone vibrated just as Daryl leaned over to top off her champagne. Reporters had been bothering her all afternoon, but she'd let them all go to voice mail. She glanced at the caller ID—Abe Monticello. Rising, she said, "I have to take this." Then she walked out onto the patio. If Richard Starkweather was using Abe's cell phone again, she was going to—

"Piper. The story's just breaking on the news here in D.C. Thanks to you, Patrick Lightman is going back to jail. Are you all right?"

Not Richard, but Abe.

"I'm fine. What do you mean thanks to me?"

"The FBI has released an official statement that you were instrumental in the arrest, and that he was trying to abduct you when you took him out with a rock. You're a heroine. Don't you watch TV up there?"

She turned back to stare at Duncan. "We've been busy." Especially Duncan, she suspected.

"I need you back here in the office on Monday. Now that you're out of danger, I want you to take over second chair on the Bronwell trial. Richard can't seem to do anything with the files you left him. Will you come back?"

"Yes," she said. "But there's something I have to take care of right now."

Then she strode into the kitchen and right over to Duncan's chair. "That was Abe Monticello. Evidently your boss called my boss and I'm supposed to report back to work on Monday. Now that I've been instrumental in the arrest of Patrick Lightman, I've gone from villain to heroine in the twenty-four-hour news cycle. So I'll be an asset sitting second chair in the Bronwell trial."

"You will. But you don't sound happy about it," Duncan said.

"I am." She just wasn't as happy as she'd thought she'd be.

"This is what you wanted, isn't it?" Duncan asked.

"Yes, it is." She remembered standing in the kitchen the evening before, telling Vi that this was exactly what she wanted. Her old life back. She'd wanted what she'd had before her apartment floor had been turned into an imitation of a crime scene. She'd wanted normal. And she still wanted to work for Abe. With all his flaws, he was the best teacher she could have at this stage of her career. But…

Piper glanced around the table and noticed three sets of interested eyes on them. She shifted her gaze back to Duncan. "We have to talk. Now." Then she turned and walked back out on the patio. When Duncan joined her, she led the way to the far end, then whirled to face him.

"We have to get this settled now once and for all. I know that you played a role in Abe's decision to call me."

When he opened his mouth to speak, she held up a hand. "Don't try to explain. And I know I should be thanking you. I am thanking you. It's what I wanted."

"The thing is, I don't need you to play white knight. I can take care of myself." And that was true. It just wasn't what she'd wanted to say.

Duncan studied her in the dimming light. She looked like a huntress again, and if he hadn't already fallen in love with her, he would have right in that moment.

Beyond one of her shoulders, he saw the sun, a large orangey-red ball, sinking slowly toward the lake. In a matter of minutes, it would be gone. And it reminded him of how quickly time passed. And of how much you could lose out on if you hesitated too long.

"I agree. You can take care of yourself, and we do need to settle this." He took her hand and drew her quickly along the path that wound through the garden. He didn't stop until they were standing beneath the stone arch.

"Okay," he said. "I think it's only appropriate to settle everything in the place where everything began between us."

"Yes." Her gaze strayed to the spot on the right side of the arch where the metal box was hidden. Then she clasped her hands together. "You're right. Everything did begin here. With that fantasy I wrote out. And…I think…I…"

Duncan narrowed his gaze on her. Had he ever seen her at a loss for words?

She twisted her fingers together and met his eyes. "I know what you're going to say. It's just…I…"

It was only the second time he'd ever seen her rattled. He'd be a fool not to take advantage of it. Stepping forward he took one of her hands and linked his fingers with hers. And just that contact had his own tension easing a bit. Keeping his eyes steady on hers, he raised her hand to his lips. "You don't know what I'm going to say, Piper. Because I'm winging it here. I don't have your way with words. But I didn't bring you here because of that fantasy you wrote all those years ago."

"You didn't?"

"No. I brought you here because I thought it was the best place to explain exactly what I want. I'm taking a page from your book, and Angus and Eleanor's book. I want to tap into every bit of the power of the stones, just as they did."

When she simply stared at him, speechless, Duncan felt one flutter of panic. But there was no way he was going to back down or revert to sitting on the sidelines. No way. "I love you, Piper."

When she continued to stare at him, the panic fluttered again. "I know you like things neat, but I can't promise you that. And I can't promise you that I'm not going to want to take care of you. Because I intend to keep doing that for a very long time."

She still said nothing, but even in the shadows, Duncan caught the sheen of tears in her eyes. Panic did more than flutter this time. It spiked through him like a spear.

When she opened her mouth to speak, he tightened his grip on her fingers. "You are not going to talk me out of this. Don't even try."

"Okay."

"Okay?"

Her smile spread slowly, and fear and panic flowed out of him just as easily as the one tear that rolled down her cheek.

"I didn't want this to happen," she said.

"Ditto." He smiled at her. "But it has. So we have to deal with it. Don't run away, Piper MacPherson."

"No, I won't. And we will deal with it, Duncan Sutherland." She rose on her toes and used her free hand to bring his face down to hers. "Together. Because I love you, too. So kiss me again beneath the stones. Might as well tap into as much of that power as we can."

He did, and as they both sank into the kiss, the stones surrounding them sighed.

* * * * *

So you think you can write?

Mills & Boon® and Harlequin® have joined forces in a global search for new authors.

It's our biggest contest yet—with the prize of being published by the world's leader in romance fiction.

In September join us for our unique Five Day Online Writing Conference **www.soyouthinkyoucanwrite.com**

Meet 50+ romance editors who want to buy your book and get ready to submit your manuscript!

So you think you can write?
Show us!

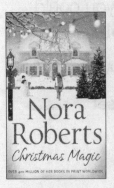

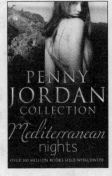